FATED FLAMES

VOLUME I

JAYLENE FORESTER

Twin Oaks
publishing

CONTENTS

To the most handsome man I know

"You don't have to do this," my mother says as we survey the port for our first look at my future husband.

I grip the ship's railing as I take in the crowd below. Even at sunset, the port we're anchored in is livelier than any at home. "We're already here."

"A better offer could still come," she says.

A sound just short of a laugh escapes my lips. "Mama..." Rarely do I call her this now, and never if servants are nearby. But for these final moments before we leave the ship, Queen Lirtha and I stand alone.

"I'm serious, Serah," she says, eyes narrowed against the glare shining off the distant desert. "This was only your first offer."

"There won't be a better one."

With surprising speed, she takes my face in her hands and turns it toward her. "For you, there is always better."

I smile at her. "For the fourth daughter of Vasna?" The entire continent knows our tiny island country is on the verge of poverty.

My mother's face remains stern. "For my daughter, yes."

Slowly, she releases me, and I am able to release my smile. We both know there will be no other offer of marriage like this. First daughters could hardly dream for what I've received.

The Dragon King, the most feared ruler on the continent, has offered to forgive all Vasna's debt. Not just the debt we owe his home country of Tirenth but *all* our debt, and thanks to my predecessors, that amount is nearly inconceivable. The only price?

A bride of royal blood with the gift of water drawing, and out of my five sisters, I alone inherited the gift, making me the sole candidate.

Right now, the only water I feel is the ocean's presence throbbing beneath me—deep and wild, cold and immense. I keep my mind focused elsewhere, for the ocean is a force never to be called upon.

Mother and I brace our legs as a wave rocks the ship. "If the stories about their kind are true..." she says.

"The stories are a lie," I answer.

I say this with a confidence I don't feel.

Dragons shed their beastly forms ages ago in favor of their secondary human bodies. They look no different than us, and they're known to be ardent lovers of logic and art. But there are stories, stories that they are still beasts behind closed doors, in their homes...in their beds...

"Still," Mother says, "you remember what I said. If he tries to harm you..."

I'm glad her attention is elsewhere so that I may roll my eyes as I repeat the words she's said so many times. "He has to sleep sometime."

"That's right. And when he does?"

My throat tightens, but I say the words she wants. "I will ensure he never wakes."

"Good. I have paid our contact there well, from my personal coffers. If you are in danger, he will see you to safety."

"I know."

"He will offer you a yellow desert rose to make himself known. Do not forget."

"How could I when you have reviewed me on this for the past two months?"

Her mouth quirks in amusement. "Then I suppose I don't need to remind you to write Selena and me as often as you can."

"You don't." I'm surprised my youngest sister has left us alone this long. She has clung to me like a little lemur for weeks now in anticipation of my leaving, as our other sisters are already married and gone. "As soon as I know it's safe, perhaps she can come visit me."

My mother is silent a moment, her eyes pinching ever so slightly as her gaze wanders. I know that faraway look. She's thinking of my father. *May the Creator keep his soul,* my lips form soundlessly, though my heart is hardly in the sentiment.

He can rot for all I care.

"Perhaps," mother says finally. Blinking, she tsks. "Where is this king of yours?"

A sudden tug at my hand draws a smile from me. I knew Selena couldn't stay away long.

"Why is it so hot?" my little sister hisses.

"It is the desert," I say, fighting to contain my amusement at her indignation. At eleven, she is already the fieriest of the family.

"Well, it's too hot."

I can't argue. The verdant jungles of our homeland are cool and shaded within. This is like standing inside an oven.

Selena leans over the ship's edge as the crew bustles about behind us. "I don't see any dragons."

On my other side, mother sighs. "Selena, we have spoken of this. Dragons look like us now."

Selena's lip pokes out. "I thought I might at least see some wings. Or horns."

Mother peers over the edge herself. "No. They don't tromp about like beasts anymore, or so I hear."

"Mother," I whisper. I've never heard her so openly impolitic.

She only shrugs a shoulder, which silences even Selena. A lady never shrugs, she says, and yet she looks wholly unrepentant for the gesture.

This will not be an easy day for her.

I set my own shoulders back as a man reeking of spirits wobbles up beside us.

"Welcome to Tirenth, Princess Serah," he bellows. My mother takes a deep, steadying breath. Selena scowls at him.

"Thank you, Minister Abely," I say in a neutral tone. Supposedly, this man is a dragon, though I can't see how. As one of Tirenth's ministers of foreign relations, he arrived in our country weeks ago and was meant to instruct me in the ways of his kind. Instead, he spent the majority of his time carousing in the local tavern, leaving me not at all impressed with the king's discernment.

As well as woefully unprepared to meet him.

Incompetent ministers aside, the day of my departure came, and I'm here now to begin the customary period of courtship. This much I do know, so I hold my head high as the gangplank is lowered and my mother, sister, and I approach it together.

"Shouldn't he be here by now?" my mother asks, squinting into the gathering crowd.

Abely, who's shaking his pocket watch, says, "Who?"

She arches an eyebrow at him. "The king?"

His hand stops. "The king..." He looks about him as if suddenly realizing where we are. Paling, he tucks the watch away. "Yes. Yes, of course, Your Majesty."

Mother and I exchange a glance as he cuts a deep bow.

Rising, Abely clears his throat and looks across the port. "Ahh, there," he says with a tilt of his head before turning away to begin mopping his face with a handkerchief.

"Where?" Mother asks.

"Just there, Your Majesty." Abely's eyes skitter over to the place he gestured to and away again. "The one with the horns."

My lungs falter.

The one with the...*what*?

Heart in my throat, I turn that direction.

And lock eyes with my betrothed, the Dragon King.

2

He's tall and well-built with shockingly white hair, which might normally draw my attention.

If not for the horns.

Black as onyx and wickedly sharp, they emerge from his hair to curve up and back, much like the illustrations of dragons I've seen deep within my meanderings through the royal library. I swallow, certain that the sound is loud enough to reach his ears.

Selena suddenly gasps out, "They're so pretty!"

"Hush," my mother says from between her teeth.

"What? They are."

Pretty isn't the word I would have chosen. Alarming, perhaps? Frightening?

Intimidating?

"This is not what we agreed on," my mother says in my ear. "Serah, say the word and I will have the captain cast off."

The king doesn't take his eyes off me, nor I him. He does not smile; there is no warm expression of welcome, and yet his gaze fixes on me with an intensity that incites a warmth in my own chest.

"No," I say slowly, "we have promised our people relief."

"Our people are strong, and they love you. They will understand this."

"I know."

Finally, I break off my gaze with the king, and picking up my skirts, set a foot on the gangplank. From behind me comes a sound like a squawk, and suddenly Minister Abely is there, sweating and apologizing.

"Please, princess, he will come for you here. Look."

I glance over. The king is indeed making his way toward me, the crowd parting before him. Strangely, I mark only two attendants following in his wake. The king of neighboring Ilanthren travels with a veritable flock of people, and Tirenth is arguably the most powerful country on the continent. Odd.

At the foot of the gangplank, his attendants stop while the king strides on. A breath later and he's standing in front of my mother. Selena and I drop into curtsies, as is proper. My mother, who should incline her head to a fellow ruler, doesn't move.

"Queen Lirtha." The king sweeps a low bow. "Thank you for bringing my bride."

His voice, pitched low, is deep yet emotionless. My mother glares down at him, her face red with rage.

"What is this?" she demands.

I suck in a breath at her address. The king straightens, the angle of the gangplank placing him at direct eye-level with her. He tucks his hands behind his back.

"You may need to elaborate, Your Majesty."

"This," Mother says, waving a hand at his horns. "My daughter came to marry a man, not a beast."

"Mother!"

"Quiet, Serah," she snaps. Turning back to the king, she raises a finger as if to scold him. "I will not allow this."

His face remains completely placid. "You will not allow my horns?"

Selena slaps her hands over her mouth as a snort of laughter bursts out.

"I will not allow my daughter to marry one such as you," Mother says. "You aimed to deceive us, and I will not stand for it."

The king's head tilts incrementally, and for a moment, I'm reminded of some fanged predator examining a particularly feisty bit of prey. A chill creeps down my spine.

"You're saying," the king drawls, "that you were unaware the ruler of Tirenth is, in fact, a dragon?"

Mother leans forward till they're nearly nose to nose. "I'm saying I don't care what fortune you hold," she hisses. "You won't have my daughter."

This, finally, evokes a reaction. His eyes flash; his face darkens. He seems to loom taller, larger. His lips peel back in a grin to reveal pointed cuspids I'd be remiss not to call fangs.

"Is that so?" The dark eyes slide to me. "And what say you, Princess Serah?"

3

My heart stutters as those searing eyes turn my way.

They seemed tame when they first fastened on me from across the port—intense, but with none of the ferocity shining through them now. I hold his gaze only by the polite mettle developed from years of etiquette training.

A lady looks one in the eye when spoken to, I remind myself. *A lady looks one in the eye when spoken to...*

At my side, my mother's glare bores into me, urging me to tell the king I'll not go with him. Stars above, where is Abely? This is the exact type of situation a minister of foreign relations should be managing, but the man seems to have disappeared amongst the crew gathered silently behind us. I feel my courage shrinking as the seconds tick by.

"Do you speak, princess?" the king asks, a smirk rising to his lips. "Or should I accept the queen's words as your own?"

Selena gasps aloud. Even I start at this unexpected rudeness.

"How dare you—" my mother begins, but to my surprise, I find myself offended enough to reciprocate the king's manner.

"I can speak very well for myself, Your Majesty," I say, gripping Selena's hand tighter. "If you are able to address me with the proper courtesy."

In an instant, all mirth falls from his face.

"I am," he says, his seriousness restored, confusing me even further.

"Enough," Mother says, and turning her head toward the crew, she addresses the captain. "Cast off immediately."

The captain does nothing to hide the disdain in his voice. "Yes, Your Majesty." He and his crew disperse as if suddenly called to war. The king watches the bustle with mild interest.

"I feel I should inform you that my subjects were eagerly awaiting the princess's arrival." He waves a hand behind him at the murmuring crowd. "A week of festivities has been planned in celebration."

"A whole week?" Selena blurts before anyone can stop her.

He glances at her. "Indeed. They've waited long for their old king to marry."

To my young sister, I'm sure he looks positively ancient, but he can hardly be much older than my own three and twenty. Of course, some would consider me past marrying age...

"Her arrival," the king continues, "fortuitously corresponds with our festival celebrating the Andrames meteor shower at the month's end, so we have extended the festivities in her honor."

Mother sends me a sharp look not to react. Though it's impossible for this king to know, my love for astronomy is no secret to her. The king goes on talking while my sister stares at him, transfixed.

"There will be a feast consisting only of Tirenth's finest desserts—"

Selena gapes. "Only desserts?"

"A masked ball—"

"A ball?"

"And on the same night, the most elaborate display of fireworks ever seen on the continent."

Her eyes swell to the size of saucers. "May I come?"

The king is opening his mouth to answer when Mother circles around me, snatches up Selena's other hand, and snaps, "Of course not. We're setting sail. Now, dragon, get off my ship."

"I believe I am on the gangplank."

Mother fumes. I don't know that I've ever seen her so out of control of herself. "Then remove yourself so that I may take my daughters back to civilization."

The king bows. "If that is your wish." And with that, he turns on his heel to go.

I blink. After all that fuss, he's simply leaving? A surprising touch of regret wells up in me.

I jump as he spins back around.

"Oh, a minor detail I forgot to mention," he says in that tepid tone again. "Should the princess return home, I will be recalling Vasna's debt."

I fall completely and utterly still as his gaze shifts to me. "Immediately."

Never have I seen my mother so stunned. Her mouth drops open. For a moment, all her lips can do is move soundlessly against one another. "You can't," she says finally. "We have a contract."

"As we did regarding my bride."

She stiffens. "You think to blackmail me?"

He only shrugs, enraging her more.

As their exchange continues, I take in the crowd. Their murmurings are growing, their eyes narrowing. How would it be to anger an entire country of dragons? Besides that, how could we possibly pay Vasna's debt to Tirenth after what my father, and his father, and the father before that have done? If I leave now, what consequences might I bring on my own people? On my little sister?

Calamity is all I can see.

"The debt is insurmountable, Your Majesty," I say softly, lifting my eyes to him. My mother quiets, as does he. "Our people will starve."

The look he returns is hard. Unyielding. "A shame."

Softness I had not expected, but consigning my people to death? I can't quite disguise my shock, yet he does not give way.

He holds a hand out to me.

I feel tossed in all directions, like a ship caught in a storm. How can I marry a man like this?

How can I afford not to?

My mother is saying something I don't even hear. I was meant to bring my people relief. I cannot allow them to suffer for my sake.

Praying for strength, I step around my mother and take the dragon's hand.

4

The king's eyes fix on mine as I touch my fingertips to his palm. The skin is rougher than I expect, and my head starts flying through thoughts of scales and where all those might be found before calming myself. It's only the skin of a man who works with his hands, another oddity, but nothing to shriek over.

"Be sure, Princess," he says in a voice just short of a growl.

I run my gaze once more along the horns, the harsh features.

"I'm sure."

He bows his head. "Then let us be off."

With that, he takes my hand in a fierce grip and begins leading me down the gangplank. Mother starts after us.

"Serah, stop and think. There are other ways—"

The king comes to a halt so fast that I thump into his back. Heat spreads across my cheeks. Every eye in the port is on us. At home, I'm known as "the quiet one." I hardly want to become "the clumsy one" here.

"She has made her decision," the king says. "You are most welcome to return for the ceremony in a month's time, Your Majesty."

Welcome to return...? Selena and I share a wide-eyed look.

"It is tradition," my mother says with barely restrained rage, "for a bride's family to remain with her until—"

"That is not our tradition, as I'm sure Minister Abely told you. You, as her guardian, have relinquished her to me. She is under my care now. My servants will restock your supplies and fetch the princess's things. I expect you to cast off as soon as they're done."

He continues on, dragging me after him. I fling a look back. Am I really to leave my family without even saying goodbye?

"Your Majesty," I say, my voice a breathy whisper, but either I'm not loud enough or he doesn't care to listen. I look once more. Tears are welling in Selena's big brown eyes.

Tradition or not, this heartlessness cannot stand.

Planting my feet, I pull back hard. Finally, he pauses.

"Your Majesty," I say as near to his ear as I dare, "please, let me say goodbye to my sister."

I hear the creak of his armored coat as his shoulders stiffen. "Tradition dictates that they leave as soon as you are given."

I gather my courage once more. "Please. I'll only be a moment."

He doesn't answer.

"Please."

His head shifts toward me. "Make it quick."

Biting my lip, I tug my hand free of his and make my way back up the gangplank. As soon as I'm within reach, Selena flings herself into my arms.

"Don't go."

I draw her close and stroke her hair. "I have to, little pufferfish."

"No you don't. Mama, tell her."

Reluctantly, I meet my mother's eyes. Her face is stiff, her chin lifted.

"You should reconsider," she says.

I shake my head. "I can't." This will give our people new life, a new beginning. She knows this.

"You can, Serah. There's—" She glances past me at the king and lowers her voice. "There's another way. Come back with me."

Slowly, I unwind Selena's arms and move to stand in front of my mother.

"If there was, you wouldn't have brought me."

When I kiss her cheek, her lip wobbles. I run my hand once more over my sister's head before returning to the king.

"Thank you," I say.

He dips his head and, without turning, holds his hand out again to me. Before I can take it, my sister's voice cuts through the stifling air.

"If you hurt her, I'll be back for you! You hear me?"

I gasp, but to my surprise, the declaration is met with chuckles by the crowd. And the king...

He turns slowly and lowers himself into a deep, solemn bow.

"Come," he says when he rises, taking my hand himself this time. I take one last look at my mother and sister before letting him lead me away.

The king's two attendants meet him at the bottom of the gangplank. Twins, I realize, though it's no wonder I didn't notice upon my first glance at the pair. One, stern-faced and burly, cuts a quick bow to me. The other grins as he bows, while simultaneously holding a recently-broken nose. Very recently, from the looks of the dried blood about his nostrils.

"Soren," the burly one says, "We need to get her out of here. Now."

Soren. Dragons often guard their given names like jewels, this much I know. Did this man just reveal the king's right in front of me?

"Wyverns?" the king asks coolly.

"Yes," the man says, his face grim. "They're coming."

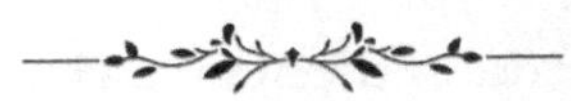

5

The king tightens his grip on my hand as if I might be thinking of bolting, which I do contemplate for a brief moment.

What's a wyvern? And why does it sound like something I'd rather not be coming?

"How far?" This the king asks the attendant with the broken nose.

I watch with open fascination as the man lifts the damaged appendage into the air to give the wind several sniffs, then flashes the king four fingers. The king answers with a curt nod.

"Clear the way, Rally," he says.

Like a great bellows, the burly attendant sucks down a breath and releases a roar of, "Make way for the king."

I catch one final glimpse of our ship before I'm being pulled through the crowd, faces blurring on either side of me.

"My things..." I begin. The king said his servants would fetch them, but I'd hoped to see them off myself. My own gowns would certainly be a comfort, but it's my books and telescope I'm more concerned with.

"They'll be brought," he says shortly.

I'm desperate to slow down, to smile at the people in greeting and make a warm impression. At this speed, I can barely make out individual features, much less exchange pleasantries with anyone. I do note the absence of any other horns like those of the man towing me along behind him. Why is he the only one?

"Make way," Rally booms again.

Noses lift as I pass, alarming me at first as I wonder if this is a sign of disapproval. I realize after a moment that they are *sniffing* me as I pass. I fight the urge to bite my lip.

"Faster, princess," the king says, giving my hand a harsh jerk.

Heat pricks the back of my eyes. My sister, Celeste, spent the first three weeks of her new marriage crying, and I'd already decided on not doing the same. Yet here I was blinking back tears on the first day. I search desperately for something to distract me.

A cat, looking out an upper window of a nearby building, catches my eye. He's a handsome tabby bearing the unimpressed expression typical of felines. A ginger watches from atop a balcony—two gingers, rather—and now that my eyes are cast higher, I note several of varying stripes and spots perched atop shoulders throughout the crowd. Cats are no strangers to ports, of course, but normally they're skulking about for bits of fish, not sitting on people as if they're chairs.

I'm suddenly wrenched to the left and we break free of the crowd, emerging onto a paved street bordered by towering stone buildings. I've barely taken notice of the carriage in front of me before the king is thrusting me up the stairs.

"Inside," he says, his hand hot against the small of my back.

The door is shut, and the carriage lurches forward.

Leaving me trapped with the king.

For a moment, he simply stands just inside, hunched and staring at the floor as if his feet took root there.

The rocking of the carriage sways his face perilously close to mine. I lean away as his nostrils flare.

Is he...smelling me, too?

A bead of sweat trickles down my back. What if I smell terrible, and he's frozen by my stench? That's ridiculous. Before the ship landed, I was bathed, powdered, and perfumed as much as one could be without risking suffocation.

Then why does he keep standing there?

I clasp my hands together in my lap, my panic growing. Again, the king inhales, the sound loud even with the rumbling of the wheels. A low growl rolls up his throat.

With great trepidation, I realize I am about to be eaten.

The idea is ludicrous, and yet I can't simply bat it away. He looks like a man, yes, and men don't eat people; yet he is a man with horns, and who knows what he drools over. I continue to lean back, but I can only lean so far.

"I've never been in a carriage," I blurt, the words tumbling out by necessity.

The king's face angles slowly toward me. My heart hitches higher at the sight of his eyes. The pupils are dilated, like a beast catching the scent of blood. I wet my lips.

"It's warmer than I expected," I add.

Just as I was taught, I imagine myself as I hope to be seen. A picture of poise. Calm and serene. Not a girl suddenly pondering which of her bones will be chewed on first.

What the king sees, I don't know, but finally—mercifully—he blinks, and blinking once more, he looks away.

"Indeed," he says, in a husky voice that sends a chill rushing over my skin.

Then he sits.

Propping an elbow on the edge of an open window, he rests his chin in one hand and taps out a rhythm on his knee with the other. I watch his fingers, too afraid to take my eyes off him entirely.

"You don't have carriages in Vasna?" he asks.

My eyes dart to his face, but he remains calm. "No, Your Majesty."

He doesn't respond. Normally, I would be more than happy to let an awkward conversation die its inevitable death. Right now, I'm eager not to fall back into the eerie display of before.

"Vasna is a tropical island," I continue. "As I'm sure you know. The landscape is not conducive for carriages. The root system is too extensive."

"Carts, then?" the king asks, still peering out the window.

Did my sisters talk of carriages and carts when they first met their future husbands? It seems a strange conversation, yet I cling to it like a barnacle on an old boat.

"We do occasionally use carts, though we tend to move goods or supplies with boats or packs worn on the back. We also train goats."

"Goats?"

He doesn't look at me, but the interest he gives this single word makes me gulp. Could a dragon eat an entire goat in one swallow? I think of my own small herd that I'd said a very painful goodbye to—Stella and Loopy, Gin and Butter. A few dragon bites would make short work of them...

I rein in my thoughts and come back to the present.

"Yes, Your Majesty. We train them to carry packs as well." Should I tell him I have my own herd? No, bad enough I sound like a yokel already, yet I can't seem to stop talking. "They're very hardy creatures. Practical for long excursions into the forest."

"And you?" The king pins me with an iron gaze. "You are royalty. How are you transported from one area to another?"

With effort, I lift my chin and answer in a steady voice. "I walk."

A knock comes on the side of the carriage. I presume from the flurry of hand signals that are given just outside the window that it's the attendant, Ty. Whatever the gestures signify makes the king grimace.

"The wyverns are waiting at the palace," he says. "There will be no avoiding them." He pauses, and his hand, which had stopped, begins its tapping again. "I'm sure Abley has informed you of the expectations."

"Ah…" My voice trails off as I think of the least offensive way to respond.

Before I can say another word, the king lunges. Gasping, I flinch back, but all that comes is a band of cold spilling across my neck.

A necklace. He's fastening a necklace.

"This is the Soul of the Sea," he says, and when I glance down, my eyes open in astonishment. An enormous sapphire in the shape of a starburst rests just below my clavicle. I've never seen a gem this size, much less worn one.

The carriage pulls to a stop. Bracing himself on the wall behind me, the king says, "The wyverns will be waiting outside." He draws back by a few degrees and pauses there, his breath sending a shiver down my neck

"Perform for me, Serah," he murmurs in my ear, "and I'll give you anything you want."

7

Per—perform for me? I focus on steadying my breaths as the king withdraws and moves to open the carriage door.

What does that even mean?

Don't be a fool, Serah, I chide myself, high color rising to my cheeks. The way between a man and woman has been explained to me in great detail, as my mother was of the opinion that these things ought not be surprises as they were for her. What else could the king be implying by his words and allowing me to wear a gem of this magnitude?

But I've only just arrived! Surely, his meaning lies elsewhere.

The Dragon King steps out and offers a hand to me, his eyes steady. I stare at the proffered hand as if it's a contractual agreement: "Here, take my hand and let us be off to the bedroom." My own hands clamp onto the underside of my seat.

The king looks at me. "Are you afraid?"

A lady does not lie, I hear in the voice of one of my tutors. *She demurs.*

"Perhaps," I say.

He cocks his head at me. "There's no need. You are with me. The wyverns would not dare touch you."

The *wyverns*. Of course. He means for me to perform well in front of the wyverns, whoever they may be. I'm flooded with relief and more than a little embarrassment.

"Ah," I say. "thank you for the reassurance, Your Majesty." Placing one hand in his, I touch the necklace with my other as I step out onto the narrow carriage steps. "And I thank you for allowing me to wear such a treasure."

He stiffens at my words. "I hope you will wear it always. It is yours now."

I'm so shocked that my foot slips, and I careen right into his arms.

The king doesn't shift an inch as my weight crashes into him. He merely catches my shoulders and goes on talking as if my cheek isn't pressed against his chest.

"I was under the impression sapphires were an acceptable choice. Have I been misinformed?"

Face burning, I peel myself off him. Not only is this my second gaffe of the day, but palace staff will surely be watching our arrival for bits of information to pass along the gossip trail. By the end of the day, I'll be known as the princess who can't walk down a slope or stairs without incident. I straighten and try to regain some dignity.

"No, Your Majesty, you were not misinformed. Sapphires are a particular favorite of mine."

"As I was told," he says, his face stern.

Who would have told him such a thing? Certainly not Abely. "Forgive me, for I was only surprised. In Vasna, such gems would only be worn by the queen, and even then, only at formal events."

I don't mention that none of the royal jewels compare with the one hanging off my neck.

"You are no longer in Vasna."

"No…"

He takes a step nearer, and as we were already close, the proximity causes my heart to beat even faster. "Are you having second thoughts, Princess?"

His voice is quiet—soft, even—and both his tone and question puzzle me.

"Pardon?"

"Do you wish to return to Vasna?" he asks.

Of course I do, I want to shout. I'm only here to help my people, and every other moment with this dragon seems like a mystery to be untangled.

Demur, Serah. Demur, demur…

"I will remain here," I say, "as was agreed upon, Your Majesty."

The king's gaze sharpens on me. "Then you accept it? The gem?"

A strange fluttering starts in my belly and trickles to my limbs as I look back at him. I almost feel I could lift my arms and soar away. Likely a reaction to the heat, I tell myself.

"I do," I say.

The king looks almost as relieved as I felt a moment ago. His shoulders relax, and an actual smile plays about his lips.

"I am most—"

"Your Majesty," a voice calls, cutting him off.

When I peer past the king, I see a trio of men, bare from the waist up, which under normal circumstances, might shock me to spot on palace grounds.

It might, if they weren't gliding down from the sky on wings as red as blood.

8

All my life, I've been told dragons could hardly even be called so anymore. After all, they only take human form and have done so for ages. They are no longer the fire-breathing creatures of myth who hoarded jewels and stole maidens.

As I watch three men descend from the sky like birds, one of them clutching a gilt-edged chest, I wonder how my education could have been so lacking.

The king reaches out to take my hand in his and I am somewhat relieved to be holding *something*. The men stalking across the courtyard are not only half-clothed, but the wings fanned out behind them are formidable. Far more than a bird's wings, they resemble a bat's, with a hand-like appendage perched at the highest point. I flush as one of the men catches me looking and uses the hand to give a cheeky wave.

Rally and Ty take up positions on either side of the king and I as the men close in. The two in the rear look to be about the same age as the king's attendants, and though the man in the lead appears only slightly older, the harsh lines about his mouth age him. And imply he does a lot of scowling.

"Soren," he says, holding his arms out in greeting. An oily smile spills over his face. "What fortuitous timing."

"Your Majesty will do fine, Lord Tallin," the king says, his tone expressionless. "May I present my betrothed, Princess Serah of Vasna."

The man's smile remains as he turns to me. His eyes flicker to the jewel at my throat and something flashes in his gaze—anger? Surprise?—before returning to my face.

"Well, well," he says. "King Soren and Princess Serah. Your names fall like a fated flame." He sweeps a bow, and the two behind him follow suit. "Had we been informed of your impending arrival, princess, we would have greeted you upon your landing. As it is, we wish to present you with a gift."

He waves the man holding a chest forward, but the man has barely raised his foot when the Dragon King says, "You'll do no such thing."

Lord Tallin looks at him with mock offense. "Whyever not? I know we have our differences, but surely, a friendly gift on such an auspicious occasion, and between old friends no less, can bring no harm."

"No."

Lord Tallin tsks. "Perhaps your future bride holds a different opinion?" With a snap of his fingers, his companions raise the chest's lid, revealing an interior brimming with glittering jewels of every color. I will my eyes not to widen at the fortune before me.

I expect the king to rebuke him, but he stays quiet. Several seconds tick by. Is he waiting for me to respond? I hardly know what I would say. My role as a fourth daughter has been to smile and serve our people by drawing water where it's needed, not engage in political rivalries. As the sun beats down, and the silence drags on, the atmosphere veers fully into awkwardness.

"She's certainly no chatterbox," Lord Tallin quips, "is she?"

My cheeks burn with indignation. Vasnan nobility is no high court; I know this. I've helped plow fields and fell timber with any number of our nobles, yet none would dare speak to a member of the royal family with such disrespect. I can't help feeling both angry and humiliated.

Pressure on my hand brings me back to the moment. It's the king, squeezing my fingers with his own.

Perhaps I'm only being fanciful, or perhaps the heat is going to my head, but the gesture seems to say, *Fire back.* Before I can doubt my interpretation, I fix the wyvern with a benign smile.

"Pardon my reticence, Lord Tallin. As I was taught many words are the mark of a fool, I thought it best to let you continue."

Lord Tallin draws back, his shock evident. The man who waved his clawed wing at me actually snickers. I keep my expression neutral, though in truth, my daring astonishes me.

"So she does have some bite," Lord Tallin says. The corner of his mouth creeps up. "How wonderful."

"Indeed," the king says, his hand firm against mine. "Now, if you'll excuse us, the day advances, and I'm sure Princess Serah would appreciate some rest."

Lord Tallin smirks. "Of course. I suppose we'll be off then." With a bow, he turns on his heel, his entourage in tow. The king watches them go.

"Oh," Lord Tallin says over his shoulder, "do let me know if you tire of your pet, Soren." The one eye angled toward us rakes over me. "She's quite lovely."

There isn't even time for disgust to take hold before a snarling blur rushes by me.

9

My hand flies over my mouth as the blur splits in two and both Rally and Ty charge the wyvern lord, his attendants whirling around with wings flared wide to face the twins. They're going to all come to blows right here in the palace courtyard on my first day in Tirenth. Over something said about *me*.

Mother would be appalled.

"Boys," the king says in a perfectly placid tone.

Rally and Ty freeze.

"We are civilized here."

The courtyard seems to pause, waiting for what will come. Lord Tallin's attendants flash their bared teeth, goading the twins, and the air, stifling hot, is thickened further by the broiling tension. I resist the urge to wipe the sweat from my brow.

With obvious reluctance, Rally and Ty step back in perfect synchronicity to stand by their king. Lord Tallin grins.

"A wise choice. There's no need for violence, is there? We seek peace."

"Is that so?" the king asks. "Historically, your terms seem to suggest otherwise."

"We believe our terms reasonable."

"Belief does not equal reality."

Lord Tallin's lips stretch till all his teeth are exposed. "No, it does not." His eyes flicking once more over me, he turns and makes to crouch down again as if preparing for flight.

"Lord Tallin," the king says, the call soft as a whisper,

The wyvern looks back and cocks an eyebrow. "Yes?"

The king doesn't charge forward or raise his voice, yet when he speaks, the quiet threat in his tone is enough to chill me to my bones.

"Insult my bride again," he says, "and I'll rip your mouth out."

Lord Tallin sneers, yet he doesn't respond.

Facing the sky, the trio extends their wings, and with a mighty flapping and a great deal of whirling dust, they take flight. I watch in muted—and begrudging—awe as they sail away.

The king watches as well, but his is a calculating gaze, like he's measuring the distance between them and us. At some predetermined height, he jerks toward Rally.

"I want her inside, in her chambers. *Now.*"

I startle at his harsh manner. Where he was all control a moment ago, now he seems seconds away from falling into a rage. In truth, I would like nothing more than to be alone in my room and sort through this wild day, but I suddenly balk at the idea of being hustled off there like a disobedient child.

What would Mother say? Probably to keep quiet until I better knew this king, his strengths, his weaknesses. My sister Celeste would likely start crying. My oldest sister would have half the palace under her command by now.

In the end, I, Serah, the quiet one, say nothing as the king drops my hand and addresses his attendants.

"I want both of you on her."

Rally steps after him as the king goes to leave. "Soren—"

"I said *both*," the king snaps before stalking away.

Ty flings his arms out in exasperation at the retreating back of his king.

"Leave it, Ty," his brother grunts. I stiffen as he rotates my way, but it's only to bow. "Shall be off, princess?"

Tired and disappointed in myself, I simply nod and follow them. At least I'll have a small look at the palace I'm to live in before evening sets in.

Instead of heading toward the main entrance, the brothers veer to the right, taking me down a covered walkway. To my surprise, the walkway's edges are lined in beds bursting with flowers, and I feel a small but steady trickle inching along beneath my feet.

"Great efforts have been made to bring water here," I say quietly.

I hadn't said the words to anyone in particular, but in response, Ty sends his brother a barrage of hand signs, making the latter scowl.

"That's hardly on the way."

I watch them exchange a great number of signs before Rally sighs.

"Ty wants to know if you'd like to see the eastern gardens. Briefly," he adds, with a cutting glance at his twin.

"Oh, yes, please," I say, my heart clinging to this small bit of normalcy. Ty grins at me, but the grin disappears as a voice emerges from the corner at my back.

"The eastern gardens first? She'll hardly want to see the others after that."

I turn slowly, my mother's teachings in my ear—*Head up. Shoulders back. Never show a man fear.* I couldn't seem to remember these words earlier in the carriage, but I grasp onto them now as the man lurking in the shadows pushes off the wall he was leaning on, and in one fluid motion, sweeps a hand down to pluck a flower.

"Everyone knows you must save the best for last," he says. Bowing, he presents the flower to me.

It's a yellow desert rose.

IO

My mother's words on the ship come rushing back to me as I stare at the proffered flower.

"He will offer you a yellow desert rose to make himself known..."

Relief washes through me. So this is my mother's contact, the one I'm meant to seek out if I'm in danger.

The man rises, revealing a strong chin and laughing eyes. He wears his long hair pulled back in a low tail much like many of the men of Vasna do, and he's younger than I imagined. As I gingerly take up the flower, Ty lifts an elbow in the man's direction and smacks it with the palm of his other hand.

"Now don't be like that," the man says, flashing a smile. "Just because I startled you doesn't mean you can be vulgar in front of a lady."

He winks at me.

Ty holds his hard look another second or two before grinning and clapping the man on the back.

"I don't know how you couldn't smell him, Ty," Rally says, folding his arms over his chest, "what with all those perfumes he wears."

The man throws his head back in a laugh. "Now you're just attacking me. Please introduce me to the princess before she thinks me as vulgar as your brother."

Ty makes another rude gesture.

"Princess Serah," Rally says, "this is Lord Lyken, the overseer of the western province. Whether or not he's vulgar I'll leave up to you."

Suppressing a smile, I incline my head to the man. "A pleasure to meet you, Lord Lyken."

Lord Lyken's face grows serious. "The pleasure is all mine, princess." Bowing again, he reaches for my hand, and when I give it, he holds it with both his, touching not his lips but his forehead to my knuckles, a greeting of deep respect in Vasna.

When he lifts his eyes to mine, a look of understanding passes between us.

"Now," he says, his jovial tone returning as he straightens, "why in all the stars' names would you two show our fair princess the eastern garden first when it is undeniably the best? Why not start with the southern?"

The brothers exchange a glance. Ty shrugs his shoulders.

"It's on the way to her chambers," Rally says with a glance behind him. "Soren wants her out of sight."

Out of sight seems far more vulgar than anything else that's been said, but I keep quiet.

Pointing at the sky, Ty holds his arms up and curls his fingers into claws while simultaneously pulling a long face that can't be anything other than Lord Tallin's sneer.

Lord Lyken's eyebrows shoot up. "The wyverns were here?"

"Just left," Rally says.

"Then I agree with the king." Pivoting to me, he holds an elbow out. "Might I join your party, princess?"

I glance at Rally, but he and Ty seem to be awaiting my approval.

"Of course," I say, glad for any brightness in a rather bleak day.

Our pace quickens, and we keep to the shadows of the walkways as we go. Despite Rally's teasing, all I smell is a faint scent of mint from Lord Lyken.

"I'm sure this has been an eventful day for you," he says quietly.

The corner of my mouth turns up. "An understatement."

"Tirenth is far different from your own homeland, I expect." His eyes slide to mine. "But I hope you'll give our humble desert a chance to charm you."

He holds my gaze for several seconds before turning forward again. I glance at him out of the corner of my eye. Is he...flirting with me? I redden. Of course he isn't. I've simply misunderstood him just as I did the king. I am here because the king wants me to draw water to his kingdom, nothing more.

"Your desert holds a unique beauty," I say, thinking back to the great, shining dunes I saw from the ship. "I look forward to seeing more of it."

"Perhaps the king will give you a tour tomorrow."

Rally snorts. "From the way he looked earlier? Doubtful."

My heart drops. Am I to be held like a prisoner in my room until the king sees fit to let me out? Normally, I can tuck my feelings away like folded gowns, but some of my distress must pass over my face because Lord Lyken's leans near.

"Give the king a few days," he whispers. "He will calm."

I nod, not as reassured as I would like. My movements have never been restricted at home. I go where I please, sometimes wandering or canoeing for half a day or more.

We come to a courtyard with a single building at the other side, a building adorned with balconies, roofed in gleaming tiles, and flanked with several guards. I sense the time for us to part drawing near.

"Please pardon me for any impoliteness," I say, "but might I ask a quick question?"

"Of course," Lord Lyken says.

"The wyverns, they are...different from dragons?"

He huffs out a laugh. "Oh yes, they are different."

"In what ways?"

"Venom, for one," Rally rumbles.

Ty springs forward a step and waves his arm behind him in a menacing manner.

"In the tail," Rally clarifies.

"I see," I say.

"And," Lord Lyken adds, "in their barbaric forms, they have two legs, not four."

In their barbaric forms...is that what they call their original bodies? It seems a sad way to refer to oneself, wyvern or no.

At the arched doors leading inside, Lord Lyken stops and bows once more.

"Until we meet again, Princess Serah," he says, and with a final wink, he's gone.

Inside is cool, and though I would like to stop and marvel at the fine marble and mosaic walls, Rally and Ty rush me up the winding stairs like a jaguar is snapping at our heels. Down a hallway and through a doorway I'm taken, until I find myself standing in a room with a balcony, a canopied bed, and a great many rugs.

"Your maid will be with you shortly, Princess," Rally says, and with that, the door shuts.

For several moments, I just stand there and breathe.

The bedchamber in front of me is larger than any I've stayed in, with several doorways leading off in different directions. The room is far larger than any my mother has stayed in even, and she's a queen.

As I am to be.

The thought causes my stomach to clench, so I distract myself by going to the balcony. To my surprise, it looks out on a small, private garden teeming with blooms and butterflies. A large fountain in the center burbles pleasantly, and I feel my tension trickle away as I listen. Whenever my things are delivered, this will be an excellent place for my telescope.

On the far side of the room, a door—one for servants, I assume—swings open, and a young woman walks in humming to herself. She's also bearing an armful of towels, which is why she doesn't see me until she's leaving the bathing chamber on her way out.

"Your Highness," she gasps. She drops into a curtsy so deep, I worry she might fall. "Forgive me. I did not know you were here yet. That is, I knew that you'd arrived, but I didn't know you were *here*, and I worried you might not have enough towels, you see..."

I give her my warmest smile as she rises. She looks to be several years my junior. "It's quite all right. Thank you for tending me so well."

The girl stares at me, eyes large in her pale face.

"Are you to be my maid?" I ask. As I've never had a dedicated maid in my life, the question feels supremely awkward, but all my married sisters have ladies' maids now; I'd steeled myself for it.

The girl points at herself. "Me? Oh, no, I'm not a maid. I mean, I am. Just not a ladies' maid, Your Highness."

"Oh," I say, trying to hide my embarrassment. "I apologize."

She looks mortified. "There's no need for you to apologize, ma'am. Not to me." Her gaze darts toward the door she came from as if she'd like to make her escape, but something catches her eye. She points a hesitant finger at the bed. "D—did you know you had a visitor?"

I glance that way in alarm but don't see anyone. Moving closer, I find a scruffy, orange tabby with notched ears spread across the end of my bed. He cracks one eye open to peer back at me.

The girl clasps her hands together. "It's so nice to be picked, and on your first day here, too."

"Picked?" I ask.

"By a cat," she says, gesturing at the tabby. "I remember the first one who picked me. Fireball. He was an orange one, too."

Cats aren't terribly common at home, as my mother isn't fond of them. Do cats generally just turn up on people's beds? "Perhaps he's only napping here?"

The girl looks doubtful. "I don't think so." She hesitates. "Maybe try petting him?"

I reach out a timid hand to stroke his head with two fingers. He leans into my touch.

"Now I'll try," she says, and when she does, the cat draws back to look at her in obvious distaste. She grins. "Well, that settles it. They're like us, you know? Once they pick someone, that's it."

A second is needed to remember that by "us," she means dragons and that *she* is a dragon. I sneak a glance at her. She looks as human as I do, of course. Everyone does, really, everyone but the wyverns.

And the king.

"Would you like me to have a bit of food and water brought for him?" she asks.

The cat rolls onto his back and stretches all four legs into the air before dropping off to sleep again.

"I suppose we better," I say, staring down at him. I could certainly do with a friend. "Thank you."

"You're very welcome, Your Highness." Curtsying again, she starts for the door.

"Oh," I call after her, "What is your name?"

She turns and smiles, revealing a gap between her two front teeth, a distinct sign of blessing in Vasna. "Cora. It's Cora, ma'am."

"It's nice to meet you, Cor—"

Like an ornery bull, a sturdy woman about my mother's age comes barging through the servant's door with a string of girls at her heels.

"You," she says, leveling a finger at Cora. "What are you doing here? Shoo!" She flaps her hands at the girl. "Shoo, shoo!"

Cora scurries out, leaving me with this formidable creature and her troops. The woman introduces herself with, "I am Hiln," and before I can say much of anything, I'm being stripped, scrubbed, and perfumed under Hiln's command. Strangely, she orders I be fed bites of fruit and cheese throughout all this as if there isn't time for a proper dinner.

This woman I can certainly believe to be a dragon.

Night has come and the lamps lit by the time they're done. The girls giggle amongst themselves as a long, silk gown lined in velvet ribbon is slipped over my head. I glance down, and my cheeks warm. The thing is nearly transparent.

"What is this?" I ask.

"Is nightgown," Hiln snaps, and with another flapping of hands, she sends the girls out, driving them before her like a flock of chickens.

When they're all gone, I sit on the bed and stare at the far wall.

My skin is raw, my hair perfumed with a scent that's making my eyes sting, and I may as well be naked with how much this so-called nightgown covers.

I will not cry. I will not cry...

I clutch the bed's edge as my resolve wavers.

All my life, I've prepared to potentially leave my home. For a brief period, I thought Luca, who I've known most my life, would offer for me, and Mother would deem a Sileshian nobleman a good enough match for a fourth daughter. But the offer never came, and the Dragon King's did.

Do not cry, I command myself. *If you start...*

It will be impossible to stop.

I look about the room for something to latch onto. At some point during all the scrubbing and scouring, someone brought and left two bowls, but when I look, the cat is nowhere to be found. I bite my lip as tears threaten to spill over.

Ultimately, it's the rug that does it. When I rub my toes against the rug beside my bed, it's silky smooth like the nightgown, not rough and worn like the jute one braided by my grandmother. A wave of homesickness crashes over me, and before I can stop myself, a sob breaks loose.

Curling onto my side, I cry. I cry over my foolishness, and my naïveté, and my cat friend who left. I cry because I'm still hungry, and I refuse to call anyone and have them see me like this. Most of all, I cry because I don't want to marry the Dragon King, but I don't want my people to starve.

I startle as something warm and wet scrapes across my hand. Lifting my head, I find a pair of glowing eyes staring back at me.

"Cat," I blub, reaching out to him. "You came back."

The wonderful creature presses himself to my side and stays there, purring, as I cry some more.

I may be the quiet one, but I am also the practical one. As I sniffle into my friend's fur, I decide I will cry this all out, and in the morning be ready to face my future again. I will hold my head high and—

I freeze at the sound of a door unlocking.

The sound came not from the direction of the servant's door, but from the opposite side of the room. Launching myself upright, I stare as a mosaic panel opens to admit a narrow strip of candlelight.

As well as the king.

My breath stills in my lungs at the sight of him. Gone is the armored coat, and the shirt that does remain is open at his chest. His boots are missing, and he appears to be working at removing his belt as he steps into the room.

"You performed admirably today," he says.

The door closes behind him with a snick.

"And I wish to thank you."

II

I'm frozen in place, completely unable to tear my eyes away, yet a thousand thoughts fly through my mind as I gape at the king.

Why is he here?

Where are his clothes?

Why is he continuing to remove his clothes?

The king, oblivious to my panic, moves deeper into the room, his glossy horns reflecting the dim light. "I apologize for my delay," he says, his attention on his belt, which seems to be snagged on something. "I needed to tend to something urgent."

He turns slightly, revealing a small pillow tucked under one arm. My heartbeat, already thunderous, throbs against my ears.

Stars above. He intends to *stay* here.

I start as he jerks the belt loose with a snap and begins winding it about his fist, the leather creaking against his hand.

"If you would kindly let me know," he says, "which side of the bed you prefer that I—"

I can hear no more. Pushing myself back, I roll off the other side of the mattress and onto my feet, immediately dropping the rest of my body into a defensive position.

The Dragon King looks at me then. Gawks, really.

"What are you doing?" he says.

I don't answer him. I'm not sure I can. My mouth seems to have stopped functioning. The cat, who has watched all this with little interest, yawns.

The king's head tilts to the side. "Why is your face wet?"

"You will answer me first," I say, my voice breathier than I wish. "What are you doing in my bedchamber?"

He gestures toward a darkened window. "It's night. Where else would I be?"

I have the sudden and uncharacteristic urge to grab my own pillow and throw it at him. "In *your* bedchamber," I snap.

He looks baffled. "Then how would the staff believe we are fated?"

What? My hands lower as my confusion overtakes my focus. "That we are what?"

Now he looks positively incredulous. He stares at me several seconds before dropping his pillow to the ground, sitting on it, and studying me as if trying to decipher some ancient tome.

"I was under the impression you understood the full terms of our arrangement," he says.

Alarm courses through me. I can't have him doubting my commitment. My people need this.

I soften my tone. "Perhaps you could remind me of the specific terms currently at play, Your Majesty."

His brow creases. "Does your palace staff not gossip?"

Why must he speak in riddles? "Of course."

"Then the same is true here, and we need them to gossip about us. My subjects will not accept a human queen, not unless we can convince them she is my fated flame."

Fated flame. Lord Tallin used the same term, though he did so in a mocking way.

"Fated flame..." I repeat.

"My heart," the king says, his gaze boring into mine. "My missing lung. My mate."

I'd love to question him on the lung analogy but don't dare. "Ah. So you wish for your staff to think you are here to..."

"To bed you."

A wave of heat rushes up my cheeks at the brazen words. I was searching for a delicate way to address it.

"We are meant to wait for the wedding," he continues, "of course. But if we are fated, it is expected that my passion overwhelm my reason, that we both be driven mad with longing. Hence, I am here."

Embarrassment clogs my throat. What am I to say to that? How am I to feel? My hands fall to my sides.

"Now that we have reviewed," the king says, adjusting his shirt sleeve, "I would be most grateful if you would tell me which side of the bed you prefer I lie next to so that I might avoid being stepped on."

I barely hear him. I'm fighting with all my reason to reconcile myself to this astonishing turn of events.

I'm to *pretend* to be his mate? His heart? His missing lung? A wife I can be, but this sounds like something far beyond that. I find myself dropping back onto the bed. "How am I to do this?" I whisper.

The king blinks perplexed eyes at me before they drift to my throat, to the glittering jewel there. "Did we not send a competent representative to train you in our ways?"

I hold my tongue at the word "train."

"Well?" he demands, a note of desperation there.

I'd nearly forgotten about Abely. After we disembarked, the man disappeared, and I hadn't thought of him since.

Sheer shock prompts me to answer the king without a trace of diplomacy. "Whether he is competent or not, I don't know. He spent nearly the entire time in the tavern."

I regret my words immediately.

Actual flames leap to life in the king's eyes. His muscles go rigid, like a predator preparing to pounce.

"What," he growls out, "did you say?"

12

I fall perfectly still at the sight of those fiery eyes aimed at me.

"I said—" A pause is needed to wet my throat. "I said Minister Abely spent his time in the tavern."

The king's mouth works as if suppressing the urge to bare his teeth. "And how much time was spent teaching you?"

Sweat prickles along the back of my neck. I can't tell if I should be striving to save myself or Abely. "I saw him the day he arrived. Perhaps once or twice more."

The king's gaze snaps once more to the necklace then back to my face. "And what knowledge did our honorable minister impart?"

My harried mind draws a blank. Surely, the man taught me *something*. I bite my lip, a nervous habit my mother had worked long to scold out of me. I look to my cat friend, who only busies himself with licking his backside.

"He let me know not to call you by your given name, Your Majesty," I say.

An eye twitch follows this admission. "What else?"

I'm forced to shake my head.

His jaw tightens. "Then you did not know…"

Whatever his next words were meant to be, he lets them drift away between us like smoke in the wind. The fire in his eyes dims. A touch of pity pricks my heart at this abrupt forlornness.

Suddenly, he shoots to his feet, causing me to jump back.

"Why was I not told about this?" he demands.

"We—we did not wish to offend you, my king."

His eyes blaze with fresh heat. For a moment, he doesn't even seem to see me his rage is so great. I fight to convince myself that the horns aren't lengthening as I watch.

"I'll kill him," the king snarls to himself. "I'll bite off his head for this." Whirling around, he stalks toward the door.

"Wait!"

I hardly realize I've come around the side of the bed, but here I stand in the middle of the room with nothing between the king and me but the wretched rug beneath my feet. He stops with his back to me.

"Your Majesty," I say, "you aren't really going to...what I mean is, surely, this can wait till tomorrow."

I have no affection for Abely and his incompetency, but I don't want to be responsible for his *death*.

"Abely has dishonored Tirenth," the king says without turning. "He has dishonored me, and he has dishonored you. One of those alone would warrant me dragging him from his bed and ripping him apart."

His voice darkens as he speaks, and fear sees me leaping in to stop this descent.

"I agree he has acted most dishonorably," I say. "But please, consider that I've only just arrived—"

"All the greater the insult."

"—and having the head bitten off one of your ministers will not endear me to your subjects."

Here, he pauses. His shoulders remain stiff, but they start to rise and fall in even measures. I begin to relax myself.

"I will kill him quietly," the king says before angling again for the door.

True panic sets in. I can't let him kill a man—a dragon, a whatever he may be—for being a ridiculous drunk! The king grabs the door handle.

"If you leave," I call out, voice quavering, "I'll tell everyone I threw you out of the room, and how will that look?"

He pulls up short. Slowly, his head turns back my way. "What?"

I clench my fists at my sides. "You heard me. I'll tell all the staff I threw you out. No one will believe we're fated fires—"

"Fated flames."

"That. No one will believe a word of it."

It's a bold move and likely foolhardy, but a realization struck me in the brief seconds between his threat and mine. Yes, I need him to pay Vasna's debt and pull my people out of poverty. I need him desperately to do so.

But he needs me, too.

His land is dry as a bone, and I sense the little water that is near dwindling. My gift carries great value here.

The king doesn't move. "Do you threaten me?" he whispers.

When I don't answer, he pivots, and in two strides, he's before me. My heart quickens. I have to crane my neck back to meet his eyes, which no longer hold flames, yet somehow seem just as piercing.

"Do you," he repeats, "threaten me, Princess?"

I want to say no. I want to crawl beneath the blankets behind me and hide away from this dragon king, from the bulk of him looming over me, but if I learned anything from my mother, it's that giving in once is a slippery slope without end.

"I'm not threatening you," I say, lowering my voice to match his. "I'm asking."

"It didn't sound like an ask."

"Then I am asking now." I resist the urge to bite my lip again. "Please stay, Your Majesty."

All my courage is needed to hold his gaze in the seconds after. I'm reminded of what I was told when I was a little girl about wild dogs, to not meet their eyes lest they take that as a challenge. Now, I stare directly into the king's, sure I'll lose if I look away.

To my shock and infinite relief, the king draws a long breath through his nose and finally—*finally*—relents. He does this by whirling around, snatching up his pillow, and flinging it onto the rug beside my bed. Then he flops down with arms crossed and lies there, looking for all the world like a sullen little boy. Rolling over, he turns his back to me.

I puzzle over him another moment before padding to the over side of the bed and climbing in. My cat friend rises to come curl against my side, and I stroke him as I stare off into the dark.

Are all dragons like this? Raging one moment and sulking the next?

"Goodnight, princess," the king grumbles.

"Goodnight, Your Majesty."

***

My eyes flutter open to the sound of a tap at the door. Blinking against a mid-morning sun, I strive to make sense of my surroundings.

Tirenth. I'm in my room in Tirenth.

My cat friend, apparently impervious to morning knocks, is nestled against my back. I can't believe I actually fell asleep with the king lying right next to—

Someone lets out a groan just behind my ear.

"Tell them five more minutes," a husky voice says, breath tickling my neck.

My eyes widen. It isn't my cat friend nestled against me. It's the king.

13

I barely manage to swallow a shriek.

The king is *in my bed*.

Throwing the blankets off, I leap from the covers and gape down at him. A second knock, a hair louder this time, sounds at the servant's door.

The king lets out another groan. "Are you going to tell them or not?"

I fling a look back at the door, panic roaring through my mind. "Tell them what?" I hiss.

With a great sigh, the king heaves himself onto his elbows. "Five more minutes," he bellows before flopping back onto his stomach. A feather, incongruously caught on the tip of one horn, flaps about like a flag as he does. I stare at it a moment before stammering out, "What are you doing here?"

"How do you not understand the meaning of five more minutes?" he grumbles into his pillow.

Of all the—

"I understand it perfectly fine," I snap, "but you haven't answered me. What are you doing here?"

He rubs an eye with his fist. "I thought we discussed that last night."

"Yes, you said for your subjects to believe us fated flames, you needed to sleep in my room, not in my bed."

The king rolls to his side to stare at me as if I'm daft. "Did you expect me to stay on the floor? The staff would think we were fighting."

"We did fight," I remind him, the sudden waking making me ornery.

"Yes," he says, stretching an arm, "because you were being unreasonable."

My mouth falls open. "Me? You wanted to kill a man last night."

"Still do."

I clamp my lips together. Best not to bring up Abely if I'm to keep him alive.

"We don't have time to discuss that right now," I say quickly. "They'll be back any minute. What are they here for anyway?"

"To serve us breakfast, of course. Are you not served breakfast at home?"

I cross my arms. "My mother doesn't take with breakfast in bed. She says it encourages laziness."

The king snorts and covers his head with a blanket. Leaning forward, I pull it back down.

"Your Majesty, please," I say. "Could you not at least get up and—and put on some clothing?"

Currently, the blankets are covering him from the neck down, but he's certainly not wearing a shirt. What if he isn't even wearing pants? The thought of the staff seeing us together in such a state turns my cheeks blistering hot.

"But I'm tired," the king whines just as I hear footsteps approaching again.

"You are the Dragon King," I whisper. "You are the most feared ruler on the continent. You cannot be too tired to get dressed!"

"Well I am."

A third knock comes. That couldn't have been five minutes. I whirl around in search of an escape. Perhaps I can hide in the dressing room.

"Do you want to convince them or not, princess?"

I turn at the king's question. He's drawn himself up into a seated position, exposing his bare chest and arms. Men often go shirtless in Vasna, and yet I stand there as if I've never seen any of them. I've certainly never seen a man with such pronounced muscles, such defined lines...

My eyes dart away.

"Stay and have breakfast with me," the king says, running a hand through his hair, "and you'll not have to see hair or hide of me for the rest of the day."

His tone is such a sudden shift that I forget he's half-clothed. I look at him again, puzzled once more by the swift change in mood. His eyes cut to my own.

"Unless you'd rather go home," he says.

Is this to always be his threat? Bolstering myself, I lift the hem of my nightdress and climb back into bed. "No, Your Majesty. We have an agreement."

My cat friend, who I hadn't noticed before now, emerges from the king's other side to enjoy a long, leisurely stretch. I purse my lips at him.

Traitor.

Facing the servant's entrance, I clear my throat and call, "Come in," but instead of that door, the one Soren entered through last night slams open. A young woman wearing more frills than dress bursts into the room, gasps at the pair of us, and levels a finger at the king.

"Soren," she cries, "how could you?"

14

I stare openly at the girl pointing at the king.

She's quite small, dainty, even. It's probable her dress makes up half her bulk, and yet the accusing finger she directs at the king carries the force of a far larger person.

The king shuts his eyes and inhales deeply. "What are you doing here, Tilly?"

He calls her by her given name? Who is this? Her red hair, style of dress, and heavy face paint all suggest she's Ilanthren, so what in the stars' names is she doing here?

Wait. My eyes glance over her again.

Could this be a lover?

I concentrate on not biting my lip. Mother had taught me long ago not to expect monogamy from any match I made; such expectations were a recipe for heartbreak, she said. No, it was better to produce an heir or two, let my husband roam, and enjoy the ensuing peace. Still, Mother hadn't said to expect a paramour to barge her way into my bedchamber the very morning after my arrival.

The girl plants her hands on her hips. "You said I'd be home before she came," she says to the king.

He yawns. "I said you might be home *if* you took care to leave on schedule rather than accepting every invitation that comes your way and losing track of time."

"Oh, but the parties, Soren," the girl says, twirling about. "The Ilanthrens throw the best ones. How could I resist?"

I stiffen as she turns to me, eyes sparkling.

"Do you like parties?" she asks. "We shall have the best time if you do. Well, by that I mean it would be fun if you do, but it's all right if you don't—"

The king cuts her off with a stern, "Manners, Tilly."

"Oh," the girl says, blushing deeply enough to make me feel sorry for her. Lowering her head, she curtsies to me.

"Princess Serah," the king says, waving a hand toward the girl, "meet my sister, Lady Tilanthia."

His *sister*. A knot in my chest unwinds itself at the word. The interaction is suddenly rendered strange but perfectly benign.

Then again, why should I care if the king had a lover before me? I'm sure I shouldn't. This isn't a love match, after all.

"It's a pleasure to meet you, Lady Tilanthia," I say, inclining my head.

When she looks up, she's positively beaming.

"I have been *dying* to meet you," she says. Flouncing over to the bed, she flops down beside me and takes my hand. "Ever since Soren told me about you I knew we were going to be friends."

I blink at her. What could he have possibly said about me other than I can draw water?

"Tilly," the king growls.

She flaps her other hand at him and scootches closer. "So do you like parties?"

Up close, I realize how rash my worry was. Lady Tilanthia can't be older than fifteen or sixteen. The face paint is lending her several years.

The king tilts his head straight back so that he might lean it on the headboard. Even so, one of his horns scrapes the wood. "Tilly, you cannot burst into someone's bedchamber and demand to know if they like parties, especially first thing in the morning."

"But we've been introduced now," she says, spotting my cat friend for the first time. She reaches out to stroke him, and though he doesn't look overly eager, he doesn't complain either. "And it's hardly first thing in the morning anymore."

"She hasn't even eaten breakfast yet," the king grouses.

"You mean that you haven't eaten breakfast," his sister says. She gives me a long-suffering look. "I do hope you can whip him into shape, Serah."

My mouth twitches with a smile at the king's exasperated sigh.

Perhaps I'm taken up with the spirit of the moment, or perhaps this little sister has made me think of my own, loosening my tongue. Whatever it is, something possesses me to say in a grave tone, "I hope so as well."

The king actually looks tempted to laugh.

Someone knocks at the outer door this time. The king lets out a long moan.

"Must the whole kingdom come visit?" he demands.

"It's probably that breakfast you were whining about," Lady Tilanthia says, and standing, she bustles to the door and opens it.

What waits on the threshold isn't breakfast.

It's Minister Abely.

15

When I saw Minister Abely yesterday, he was inebriated but well-groomed, boisterous but reasonably collected. Now?

I've never seen a man look so haggard in my life.

The clothes are the same, but the embroidered Vasnan overshirt and loose trousers are rumpled and sweat-stained. There are dark circles under his eyes, and his hair looks as if a typhoon took hold of it.

This is when I remember his reaction upon seeing the king at the port. The minister's jovial composure had melted away in an instant, and he disappeared soon after. One look at his paling face tells me he wasn't expecting the king to be here for this reemergence.

"Your Majesty," Abely stammers, plunging into a bow. "Your Highnesses."

The king is silent. Even Lady Tilanthia appears taken aback, and to my surprise, she looks to me, as if for direction. I hesitate. Isn't this the king's place to speak first? Do I really want him to when he's threatened to kill the man?

As usual, I fall back on politeness.

"Minister Abely," I say. "Please come in. How may we help you?"

I can't believe I'm inviting this man into my room when I haven't even risen from bed, but I don't know what else to do. When Lady Tilanthia's eyes dart toward the door and back, I give a slight nod to let her know she should escape while she can, and quick as a fox, she flees from the room, which is exactly what I want to do, not only to escape this encounter but the stifling heat.

When did it become so warm?

The man comes trembling forward. He wrings his hands a moment or two. Then, to my shock, he crashes to his knees.

Oh dear.

"Your Highness," he says, glancing up at me once before dropping his head, "I've come to beg your forgiveness."

Before I can think how to respond, he bows even lower, pressing his forehead to the floor. I start to protest, but he's already speaking again. "I shirked my responsibilities," he says, "shamed my country, disgraced my king and my future queen. I am a wyrm, Your Highness, a wretched wyrm."

I blink at this strange addendum, and at the confession itself. The man certainly owes me an apology, but groveling isn't necessary.

"I should never have set foot in the tavern," he continues, as if he's the lowest soul on the continent. "I told myself it would benefit you if I better understood Vasnan culture, but I didn't realize...I should have known—"

His words break off in a sob.

I bite my lip at the sound of Abely's weeping. The sound is wholly genuine, and though I may have been frustrated with him, compassion now overrules that. Vasnan spirits are notoriously strong; Abely isn't the first to fall under their spell.

The king still hasn't said anything, but surely he can see the apology is heartfelt. Even so, it seems he wants me to respond, if his silence is any indication.

What would Mother say? No, she had no patience for Abely.

Cassandra? No, my oldest sister would probably toss her hair and have him beg some more.

I take a deep breath. I'll simply have to do my best.

"Minister Abely," I say, "I thank you for your apology. As we say in Vasna, the ocean washes all away. Let us let bygones be bygones and—"

A growl, savage and low, cuts through my words. Turning my head in alarm, I find the king staring straight ahead as if in a trance, yet his hands clench the blankets in a white-knuckled grip. Heat pours off him in visible waves, like the mouth of an oven.

"*You dare show your face here?*" he hisses.

When he turns toward Abely, the flames that sweep over the king's eyes don't catch me by surprise this time.

But the cascade of scales breaking out over his arms certainly does.

16

The scales rippling down the king's arms are bone white, yet they glisten like pearls, and for a moment, I'm transfixed by their startling beauty.

Then the king leaps.

I suppose he flings the blankets off first, of course. He might even crouch to gather his muscles or glance over the bed to gauge the distance from him to Abely's huddled form. I don't see any of that. There's only a snarling blur passing over me, followed by a hiss from my cat friend at being disturbed.

I yelp as the king's feet hit the floor like a thunderclap.

"You knew the risks," he says, his voice dangerously low. My heart leaps to my throat at the sound of it.

The risks of what? Failing? Not preparing me adequately?

Abely, sweat coursing down his upturned face, cowers. "I did, Your Majesty. I did not think the effects would be so extreme. I let my guard down."

"We are dragons. We cannot afford to *let our guard down*."

"Yes, Your Majesty."

Something about Abely's obsequiousness seems to enrage the king even further. He begins prowling back and forth like a caged animal, scales rising along his shoulders now. I startle as his flaming eyes cut to me, as they skip from my face to the jewel still at my throat.

Under the weight of that stare, I fight not to cower myself.

Flinging his gaze away, the king whirls on Abely. "Look at what you've done," he roars, thrusting a finger my way.

Minister Abely eyes lift in jerky motions to take me in as the king did—face first, then jewel. His own face blanches.

"I'm sorry," he whispers, pity in his look, not for me but for the *king*. "I'm so sorry."

Chills skitter across my skin at the sound of the king's laugh. It's no longer human.

"Sorry?" he says in a voice that rattles the windows. "You will be."

Spines assemble down his back; his horns lengthen. He is going to transform right here in my bedchamber. Abely only lowers his head, a strange stillness overcoming him. That's when I remember the exact phrasing of the king's threat last night.

"I'll bite off his head for this."

Oh no.

I'm frozen in place. My cat friend, unbothered by the prospect of a man being beheaded, lifts a leg to lick his toes. Surely, someone will knock at the door any second. The long awaited breakfast will come. Someone will arrive to say, "Sir, you cannot bite a man's head off in your betrothed's room. Truly, you cannot bite a man's head off at all."

That's what I tell myself as the king's shadow stretches long. I tell myself that till I can't anymore.

Then I leap.

Tumble is probably the better word for what I do. My foot catches in the sheets, and I nearly fall on my face before scrambling up, lunging in front of Abely, and throwing my arms out.

"Stop," I say, and that's all, because I can't think of anything else. All words vanish from my mind as I look at the king.

Scales run from temple to jawline, and his pupils have narrowed to black slits amidst the flames. The horns are far too long, and the twin points of his upper canines dimple his lips. I can't decide if I'm looking at a beast trapped in a man's body or a man trapped in a beast's.

I shudder.

The king doesn't say anything, but the breath he drags in through his nostrils is loud enough to echo throughout the room.

"Move," he grates out.

I shake my head.

His dark gaze travels down my neck to rest once again on the blue starburst glittering there. Perhaps he regrets giving me such a gift? Perhaps he wants it back? I'd happily do so to end this.

His eyes fall lower and then glance away, jaw hardening.

I stiffen as he spins around, stalks to the other side of the bed, and veers into the dressing room. When he emerges, he storms his way back with something balled in his fist, his gaze somehow even angrier. He stops mere feet from me. Fast as a whip, his hand lashes out.

I flinch.

A beat of utter silence follows. When no blow lands, I open my eyes to find round pupils staring back at me out of a scaleless face.

A scaleless, stricken face.

For several seconds, we regard one another like that, our emotions bared out of sudden surprise. When he turns his attention to the object held out beneath my nose, I do the same. It's a robe, a silk, lavender robe.

Only then do I remember the sheer nightgown Hiln, and her giggling girls, dressed me in. A deep blush blooms across my cheeks. I take the proffered robe and wrestle my arms in the sleeves, humiliation making me clumsy.

"Get out, Abely," the king says, his words flat.

The minister scurries from the room. Only when the door latches and Abely's panicked steps fade away does the king stride to a chair, snatch up the neatly folded shirt there, and exit the room himself.

I stand where I am, listening to the sound of my own breathing.

Someone raps at the servant's door. When I answer, a young maid pokes her head through to beam at me.

"Would you like breakfast now, Your Highness?"

I can't imagine eating right now.

"Yes," I say, folding my hands in front of me. "I think I would."

17

She thought I was going to hurt her. I could see it in her eyes.

The rage burning in my chest blazes higher as I pace the floor of my room. I had to leave, had to *breathe*, and yet the urge to charge back in there and demand she tell me who made her afraid of an outstretched hand is nearly uncontrollable. A female doesn't fear being struck unless someone strikes her first.

I'll tear apart whoever did it, rumbles through my mind. *I'll sink my teeth into their flesh, and rip their—*

I stop in place and inhale, lifting my hands to my chest and easing them back down as I exhale. I do this ten times before my teeth start grinding against one another.

This isn't working.

I fling my arms down and fall back to pacing. Thanks to Abely, I'm starving, which only enrages me further. How dare he come to her room and beg like some kind of victim? And while she was in her nightdress, no less. My nostrils flare. I could track his scent right now if I wanted. The smell of fear was thick on him. I could follow that...*seize him in my jaws, and—*

"I am king," I say aloud to the urge. Like a disgruntled cat, my first form curls into grumbling submission within me. I can't remember the last time I've had to remind it of its master.

I'm too close to her; that's why my control is slipping. I can smell her scent still lingering on my skin, a heady mix of jasmine and vanilla that reminds me of the glossy festival cakes street vendors sell for the Andrames shower.

I love those cakes. I want one right now. I want it slathered in icing that glistens like her skin did in the setting sun yesterday. I want to trace each glowing line with my mouth, each shining inch of—

I let out a groan and grab at my hair.

How does anyone survive this madness?

Snarling to myself, I charge from the room. The guards by her door flick their eyes my way but wisely stay in position. All of them but one. This one slips behind me like a shadow.

"On her," I growl over my shoulder.

He keeps following.

I wait until we're alone in a back corridor before swinging around, teeth bared, scales itching to rise. "What don't you understand about that order?"

Rally doesn't blink. "Princess Serah is well-guarded," he says in a maddeningly rational voice. "You're dangerous right now."

I seize the neck of his shirt. "I would never harm her, you—"

"Dangerous to *yourself*," Rally clarifies.

My jaw clenches. I endure his infuriating calm as long as I can stomach before flinging him off.

"Why did you let Abely in her room?" I demand.

"Ty did."

"And why did Ty see fit to let the minister into my betrothed's bedchamber?"

A trace of uncertainty crosses his face. "He didn't. He let Abely into her parlor and told him to wait there."

"And tell me, Rally," I say, my voice nearing a hiss, "did Abely wait there?"

My guard and most trusted comrade, my oldest friend, meets my glare with an insufficient degree of fear few would dare. "No."

"No!" I begin pacing once more, the close quarters only piling fuel on my fury. "He had the audacity to crawl into his future queen's room, to grovel like a wyrm on her floor before she was even dressed."

"He would never have hurt her, Soren."

"Of course not," I spit. Abely is like a second father to him and Ty. I know that. "But the—the..." I fight for the right word to encompass the error. "—*impropriety* of it."

If she thought Tirenth uncouth before, she'll think us barbarous by now. Her mother would sneer and call us all beasts, the tyrannical old bat.

"It was wrong of him," Rally says. The heel of his boot scrapes at the floor. "My understanding is he was in fear for his life."

"As he should have been," I roar.

A single, prolonged blink is all the surprise Rally shows. I turn from him and press my forehead against the stone wall. Half a minute passes.

"He didn't tell her anything, Rally," I say. "Nothing. He was too busy marinating himself in spirits."

This surprise actually drags a sound out of him. "Abely?"

I nod, the stone grating against my skin.

"Abely's no fool, Soren. He knows the risks."

"We all do." Yet Abely had risked losing control of himself. He risked transforming in the middle of a Vasnan tavern, risked those people's safety and my subjects' hope of water.

He'd risked me losing my fated flame before she was even mine.

Rally's disbelief is clear in his tone. "There has to be more to it."

"Or maybe," I say, my voice cutting even to my ears, "he's just not the saint you seem to think he is, hmm?"

When Rally doesn't answer, I cast a look back. His expression is stony, which tells me I cut too deep. I let out a long breath.

"My apologies," I say.

Rally lowers his head in acknowledgement.

"Look into it if you want," I say, pushing away from the wall. "But not at the risk of her safety, understand?"

"Of course. Thank you."

Silence fills the corridor. I relish the momentary quiet in my mind.

"What are you going to do with him?" Rally asks, boring into my peace.

"I wanted to rip his head from his body, but the lady disagreed."

Rally says nothing.

"I think I would have only maimed him," I say.

"You think?"

I shrug.

Rally's brows draw together in thought. "He really didn't tell her anything?"

"Other than to not call me by my name, no." A dragon's name is his to give, of course, but I'd empty my coffers to hear my name on her lips. I'd shower her in diamonds, wreath her in—

"Nothing else?"

With effort, I focus on Rally. "No."

"So she won't know what you did to—"

"No," I say firmly.

"And she's already accepted the jewel?"

I shut my eyes. "Yes."

Our heads lift at the sound of three drawn-out horn blasts, the call of visiting dignitaries arriving. I sigh.

"I'll handle it," Rally says, and when I let out a noncommittal grumble he adds, "You aren't even dressed."

"I haven't had breakfast either."

He chuckles. "You have plenty of time. They're not here to see you. They just want a look at that water magic of hers—"

My first form rounds on him before I can even think. He's half a head taller, but suddenly I loom over him, my teeth bared, my voice thick with flames.

"She's mine."

The words reverberate with enough force to rattle bones.

Rally drops to his knees, and shutting his eyes, he tilts his head back to expose his throat. It's the stance of a dragon in abject submission.

"I was not thinking," he whispers. "Forgive me, Soren."

Seeing him like that hits me like a blow. I step back, driving my first form back down as I do.

"For stars' sake," I say, glancing off, "stand up."

Rally climbs to his feet as I scrub my face with a hand. I need to go. "Was this how it was when you met Marta?"

Rally married a human female. Perhaps their kind holds some special gift for bewitching dragons.

"It wasn't this severe," he says, dusting off his knees. "I also wasn't trying to hold my horns." He makes a vague gesture toward my head.

"You know why I must."

"I do."

Turning on my heel, I go to leave. "Make sure the dignitaries are seen to properly, Rally."

"Of course, Your Majesty." A pause follows, and then, "Where are you going?"

"To find breakfast."

18

The breakfast that arrives is the strangest I've ever seen.

First, it's a veritable feast. When maids began filing into the room, I'd climbed back into bed where the king claimed to take breakfast. There, a tray with enough food to feed all four of my sisters is set up over my lap.

Second, there is so much *chocolate*. Chocolate drizzled over fruit, chocolate ganache peeking out from pastries, even a warm chocolate drink in lieu of milk or juice.

Surely, this is a special meal and not how the king eats every day?

"Is the food not to your liking, Your Highness?" This comes from a young maid straightening the blankets at my feet. She looks rather anxious over my hesitation.

"Oh, no." I smile at her. "It all looks delicious. Please thank the cooks for me." I take a bite of what appears to be a chocolate-covered mango slice to reassure her.

It is good.

The maid smiles back and returns to her work.

Two other maids—one of whom is Cora, the one I mistook for a ladies' maid—seem to be in a quiet debate, and my bed straightener joins them as I sneak glances their way. The debate seems to be over what to do with a second tray, which I can only assume to be the king's.

It seems they did expect to find him here.

I glance aside, my mouth working mechanically as I think back on the king's expression when I flinched. He looked *pained*, leaving me with the uncomfortable sensation I had hurt him far more than I feared he would me.

I didn't mean to react like that. It was only reflex, a reaction brought on by memories of—

I turn my thoughts back to my breakfast and bite clear through an oversized date.

The maids seem to be concluding the second tray should be taken elsewhere. The girl carrying it starts for the door, and I watch with unexpected apprehension. The king wanted the staff to gossip about us. They'll hardly do so like this.

"Pardon," I find myself saying.

The girls whip around. I don't need to conjure any demure flush at what I'm about to say. Heat is already climbing my neck.

"Might you leave the other tray here?" I say, my eyes fluttering to the empty spot beside me. "I imagine his majesty might be rather hungry this morning."

One of the maids is forced to conceal her smile behind a hand.

"Of course, Your Highness," says the girl bearing the tray. She fairly flies to deliver the food. Cora meets my eye and grins.

I want to hide beneath the covers and never come out.

Soon after, one of the maids finds the king's coiled belt, sealing the deal. The girls giggle and whisper to one another when they think I'm not looking, and I consider how one might tunnel into a mattress and live there.

I'm actually grateful when Hiln arrives with her bullish efficiency. She scatters the girls with a single look.

"You," she says to me. "Time to get dressed."

Once again, I'm stripped, scrubbed, and perfumed before being dressed in a silk gown embroidered with a stunning geometric pattern down the middle. My hair is pulled into an updo that is far too tight, and then Hiln and her troops disappear.

I sit and breathe in the quiet.

Everyone gone, my cat friend slinks out from under the bed. Someone seems to have filled his bowls again, which pleases me. I wonder if it was Cora. I pet the cat for some minutes before wondering, what now?

No one mentioned any events I should prepare for. I don't think I'll be called on here to tend any goats or help villagers thatch roofs.

What am I to do with myself?

There's a fine writing desk by a window, so I pen a letter to my mother and another to Selena. Afterward, I look about the room, my brow furrowing.

Where are my things?

I check the dressing room first. None of my trunks are there. It's silly, but I check the bathing room even though I know it contains little else but the continent's largest bathtub. I even wander out onto the balcony.

I puzzle over my missing things as I look over the garden below. It really is an exquisite space, filled with blooms of every shade. It must have taken ages to improve the soil enough to sustain such flowers. I wonder how the water is brought in...

A glint of light halfway up a wall catches my eye. My gaze swings that way, and my blood runs cold.

An archer stands on the balcony across from mine, his arrow nocked.

19

Instinct takes over at the sight of the arrow's point. With-out thinking, I lunge back into the room and flatten myself on the adjacent wall, chest heaving as I anticipate an arrow striking the balcony door.

Instead, the door to my bedchamber bursts open. I stare with wide eyes as Rally and Ty charge in, each of them wielding a pair of curved blades. Immediately, Rally is in front of me and Ty prowling the room.

"What is it, Your Highness?" Rally asks. He turns a slow circle in front of me, his eyes seeking threats.

"There's an archer," I say, fighting to steady my breath-ing, "on the balcony at ten o' clock. Gray clothing. Perhaps two inches shy of six feet tall."

They both turn to blink at me. I avert my gaze before they see the mote of pride there.

I was never Mother's best pupil, but even she would be pleased with my swift assessment.

Rally lowers his weapons. "An archer?"

I nod. "Yes. His arrow is nocked."

Brow still furrowed, Rally sheathes his swords and moves toward the balcony. I grab at his sleeve.

"His arrow is *ready*," I cry. Does he not know what nocked means?

I startle as Ty lays a gentle hand on my shoulder. The smile he gives me clearly says, *It's all right*, and his brother, though unsmiling, seems of the same opinion.

Are they mad?

With great reservation, I release Rally. I watch as he steps within the archer's sight.

As he lifts an arm and waves.

"Esino is one of Tirenth's best archers, Your Highness," Rally says. Dropping the arm, he comes back inside. "You have nothing to fear."

Nothing to fear? I push myself off the wall. "The man's arrow was ready to fly."

"His Majesty requires them to always be at the ready."

Them? Rally must misinterpret my expression, for he says, "No fewer than six of Tirenth's finest archers watch over your garden at any given time, Your Highness." His chest puffs out a little. "Don't worry. You are well-protected here."

Ty nods along with all of this.

Six archers? Watching this one garden? I gape at the pleased pair in front of me.

"Why would I be worried to walk onto the balcony of my own room?" I ask, my voice somewhere between whisper and wheeze. "Why would I need six archers to oversee that?"

Here, Rally pauses. "His majesty wished for you to feel secure," he says finally.

My mouth works in an effort to produce an acceptable response. "How thoughtful of him. Perhaps we could ask the archers to wait until a threat is seen to nock their arrows."

Both start shifting around as if I suggested we sit down and braid one another's hair.

"I'm afraid we would need to ask the king," is the reply.

Deep breaths, Serah. "Very well."

More shifting about follows. "If you don't require anything else," Rally says, his voice trailing off. Ty is already slinking toward the door.

"Wait, please," I say, starting after them. "I've yet to hear...what I mean is..." I'm sure they aren't the ones I should ask, but theirs are the most familiar faces. I struggle not to bite my lip. "Do you know of my engagements? What I'm meant to be doing?"

Rally looks relieved. "A feast is to be held in your honor tomorrow evening, Your Highness."

"But today...?"

"Ah, I believe the king thought you would enjoy resting today."

My cat friend comes to wind himself around my ankles. "That's very kind of his majesty," I say as I bend to pet my friend, "but I'm not tired. I would prefer to tour the palace, or perhaps meet some of the...people of Tirenth."

The brothers' eyes dart toward one another, reminding me of two children set on not revealing a guilty friend.

I am a hundred percent confident I know who that friend is.

"We'll be right back," Rally says, and before I can argue, they bolt from the room.

I stand there in stunned silence as my cat friend rubs his face on my leg. "Did you think that strange?" I ask him.

He answers by strutting to the band of sunlight streaming in from the balcony and flopping over on his side there.

"At least one of us is unbothered," I grumble.

To his displeasure, I close the double doors and draw the curtains over the glass. That done, I look about for something to occupy me until Rally and Ty return. Unfortunately, what I find is the king's untouched breakfast. If I leave it there like that, the staff will know he didn't return. That might spark rumors regarding this whole fated flames thing.

I sigh and start eating.

A quarter of an hour passes before a knock sounds at the door and I'm forced to gulp down the last of a chocolate-drenched muffin.

"Come in," I call, swiping at my face as I stand.

To my surprise, it isn't Rally or Ty. It's an older man whose granite-like face and hooked nose remind me eerily of our household manager at home.

"Your Highness," the man says as he bows at what appears to be a perfect right angle. "I am Oiken, the king's majordomo."

Of course he is.

"Would you kindly follow me?" Oiken says.

He leads me into the front room, which is set up like a parlor. I came this way when I arrived, but Rally and Ty moved me through so quickly that I only caught a glimpse. Now I see that the room seems designed for playing cards and embroidering for hours on end, both of which I loathe.

Rally and Ty, looking a hair out of breath, stand by the door leading to the hallway, and in front of a large window stands a Vasnan loom.

"A gift," Oiken says, "from his majesty."

I glance at the brothers, who are both watching me with unchecked hope in their eyes.

"How kind," I say.

Oiken looks at me expectantly. Does he want me to sit down and start weaving now? Perhaps it's only the strange morning making me contrary, but instead of dutifully moving to the chair set out for me, I smile.

"I'm afraid I hold no talent for the loom, sir."

To my surprise, Oiken seems unperturbed. He merely turns to the brothers and nods his head, sending Rally lunging out of the room.

What is going on?

No one speaks in the moments after. I send Ty a questioning look, but he only answers with a watery smile. Oiken, hands tucked behind his back, stares at the wall.

In mere moments, Rally returns with a flock of girls bearing vases of flowers. They swarm into the room, set their loads on a table, and swarm out. I sneeze.

"Perhaps you might enjoy flower arranging," Oiken says, squinting as he tries to repel his own sneeze.

"I fear I never attempted it," I say slowly.

His nose lifts. "It is a common lady's art."

I'm not confrontational, but the barb stings. "Perhaps I am uncommon," I murmur.

Oiken flushes. "Of course, Your Highness." Another nod is aimed Rally's way, and the man flees the room once more.

All through the morning, new diversions arrive for Oiken to entice me with.

"Painting, Your Highness?"

"It never took," I say.

"Perfume making?"

"I'm afraid not."

"Chocolate sculpting?"

"No thank you."

A steady stream of servants pour in and out of the room, and soon every flat surface is covered in failed attempts. With each new arrival, my resolve hardens.

The king is trying to keep me here, like a pet, and I refuse to be entertained by the toys he's sent to amuse me.

"Not there," Oiken snaps at a boy carrying a stringed instrument taller than himself. The majordomo is finally starting to crack. His forehead gleams with sweat. "Put it—no. Not there. By all the stars...over *there*, boy!"

The poor boy turns, strikes the man behind him, and the pair careens into an enormous canvas set on an easel, sending the whole apparatus crashing to the floor. The room falls silent.

That is until my cat friend knocks one of the flower vases to the floor, shattering it.

Cassandra, I think to myself. *My sister Cassandra would do perfectly for the moment.*

"Oh," I say, bringing a hand to my forehead, "I fear the crowded room is making me faint. Might we take a break?"

Oiken storms from the room, and I do try not to revel too much in his defeat. I smile warmly at the rest of the servants as they trickle out.

"Thank you for your assistance," I say. "Yes, thank you so much for your help."

My smile disappears as soon as I spot Rally and Ty trying to sneak out with everyone else.

"Wait," I say without an ounce of timidity this time. I march up to the pair of them, who stand a full head and a half higher than me, and glare. "Take me to him right now."

Ty pantomimes begging for my mercy. Rally sags with defeat.

"We've been ordered not to let you leave, Your Highness," he says.

So it's exactly as I thought. "Then bring him to me," I say. "It's either that or you'll have to lay hands on me to keep me from marching out of this room."

The threat borders on petulance, but for stars' sake, if I'm to be queen, I can't stay here all day. The very idea of being trapped like that terrifies me.

"You go," Rally says to his brother, shoving him toward the door. "I had to deal with him earlier."

Ty scowls, but he does go. Rally, after opening his mouth a time or two, decides on not saying anything at all and steps out behind his brother.

I stand amid the broken glass and wait.

My resolve wavers as a single pair of footsteps thunders up the hallway. I swear the floor trembles.

He's coming.

The knock that precedes him is polite. Controlled. I take heart from this as I call for him to enter.

The king doesn't spare a glance for the chaos surrounding us as he slips into the room. His eyes latch onto mine and stay there, making my pulse gallop.

"My guards tell me you wish to leave your chambers," he says.

His tone is perfectly neutral.

I lift my chin. "Indeed. I wish to—"

He cuts through my wishes with a single word of absolute decisiveness:

"No."

20

I blink at the man—the dragon?—the *king* who will be my husband. How can he say no when I haven't even finished my sentence?

"Pardon me, Your Majesty," I say, rolling my lips together, weighing my words like stones for those that will make the smallest ripples, "but I did not complete my request."

The king crosses his arms over his broad chest, the leather of his armored coat creaking at the folds. "There was no need, Princess. You already have my answer."

My lips part at this. Behind me, water from the broken vase plinks onto the floor.

Plink, plink.

"Is there anything else?" he asks.

I shake myself. Of course there is.

"Yes," I say. I lace my hands in front of me in the very picture of calm. "Though you have clearly considered the matter, I would be most grateful, Your Majesty, if I could make my request fully known."

This prompts a slight narrowing of his eyes, not out of anger, but confusion.

"If you must," he says, as if pondering some complex riddle. I take a deep, steadying breath.

"I am requesting to tour the palace," I say. Better to start small. "If there are concerns regarding my safety, surely a guard can accompany me."

The king says nothing.

Perhaps he's worried I'll make a run for it, a ridiculous notion, but all the same I add, "I will not leave the grounds. You have my word."

He offers no reaction. My cheeks warm as I wait.

Plink, plink.

"Is that all?" he says after several seconds of silence.

"Yes. I simply wish to see the palace. Perhaps meet some of the staff. I would particularly like to thank the cooks for the...elaborate breakfast."

His eye twitches.

"No," he says.

"No to thanking the cooks?"

"To all of it."

This time, my mouth falls open; I can't help it. Never in my life have I been told I can't go somewhere if I please. There were engagements to be kept, of course. Expectations to be met. Crops to be planted and prayed over in hopes the next typhoon wouldn't wash them away. But my free time was my own. I wandered, I roamed, I chased the sun in my little canoe.

He cannot keep me in this room. Already, I feel a cold sweat creeping over me.

"I am a princess of Vasna," I say, alarm making my voice climb.

"Indeed you are—"

Plink, plink.

"—and I am your king," he says. "Here, my word stands."

Plink, plink, plink. I close my eyes and try to shut out the sound. One should never draw water when angry.

"I will go mad," I say.

"From staying in your room?" He sounds thoroughly unimpressed.

"From being kept here like a prisoner."

"You are not a prisoner."

My eyes spring open. "Then when might I exit my chambers, *Your Majesty*?"

Instead of answering, his gaze wanders over the room and its absurd contents. "Did none of this please you? You need only name what else you would like sent."

"What I would like," I say, enunciating each word with precision, "is a bit of fresh air, sire."

"There is the balcony."

"That is watched by half a dozen archers!"

A slight crease appears between his brows. Again, I'm scrutinized like a riddle without answer. "And should a treasure not be guarded?"

I flinch despite myself. Yes, water drawing has always been a rare gift of exceptional value that guarantees a host of suitors and marriage offers for any holder.

Any holder but me.

I don't wish to think back on how my older sisters giggled over who might offer first before no one did, or how Selena scowled over the thought of me leaving until it seemed I might not at all. Or how Luca lifted his eyes so shyly to mine when we first met again at my presentation ball. I wasn't silly enough to think my regard for him was love, not when we'd seen each other so rarely through the years, but he was kind, creative, humble. Perhaps, given time, the two of us would have...

It doesn't matter now, and yet my heart yearns to return to that night of the ball, of stars racing overhead, of salt on my skin and the ocean's hum in my ears. My heart yearns to return home, really, and the sudden throb of homesickness is enough to make my eyes sting.

"Where are my things?" I murmur.

In all the hubbub, I'd still not seen my trunks. I push a bit of broken glass away with my foot. I don't want gifts. I want my books and my telescope, familiar things.

The king's answer is so long in coming that I'm forced to look at him. He isn't looking at me.

"Your things," he says, eyes fixed somewhere above my head, "are being inspected. They will be returned once that is complete."

"Inspected? For what?"

"Anything that might be a threat, of course."

I thought all my anger was gone, but it seems I held some in reserve. "What threat? Everything in my trunks came directly from my home, from my room no less."

His eyes cut to mine. "You never know where a threat may lurk."

I have half a mind to reach out and shake him. "Unless you consider gowns and books dangerous, there is nothing to warrant concern."

He frowns. "What type of books?"

I actually groan.

"You said I need only name what I want sent," I say, leveling my voice out with great effort. "Well, I want my telescope, and it is in my trunks."

"I have a better telescope," he says.

"I don't care. I want mine, and I want to leave this room." I point at the floor for emphasis. His gaze follows my gesture and lingers there for such an irritatingly long time that I look, too.

We're standing in a swirling pool of water. In my anger, I've drawn all the water from the flower vases here. I've likely drawn it from all the flowers, too, leaving nothing but shriveled up husks behind me. My mouth purses.

I hadn't meant to show him any magic until Vasna's debt was formally paid following the ceremony. As the king is facing the room, he must have watched it the whole time.

"As you can see," I say before he can speak and manage to enrage me further, "I am not accustomed to being kept indoors. I ask again, when might I leave my chambers?"

The king takes a single step nearer, making my lips purse even more.

"You may leave," he says, "when you are with me."

Water churns against my ankles now. I'm trembling with outrage. "You cannot keep me locked in here. You cannot keep me like some—some jewel in a box."

I gasp as he slips a finger beneath my chin. The seething water stills. The room falls silent. Some irrationally logical part of my brain notes once more that his skin is rougher than I would expect from a king.

He smiles then, and though there are no scales or flames, the smile that curls his lips—the hunger there, the *possessiveness*—is somehow more dragon than anything I've seen. I freeze in his grasp.

"That is exactly what I intend to do," he whispers.

And before I can sputter out a response, he releases me and walks out.

"You said *what*?"

I barely register Rally's question. It is a glorious afternoon to walk the palace ramparts, to take in the grand city beyond, which holds my subjects secure, and the palace within, which holds my princess so tightly. My mouth twitches.

Yes, it is a glorious day indeed.

We pass a guard, who drops into a low bow, and once we're out of earshot, Rally says something I don't catch.

"Hm?" I say. "What was that?"

His nostrils flare from the force of the breath he draws. He seems exasperated for some reason. "I asked what you said to the princess before walking out and leaving her locked in her room."

"Oh." I gaze out at a distant cloud. What a beautiful sight a cloud is. "I said that guarding her like a jewel is exactly what I intend to do."

My mood was foul after Abely robbed me of a leisurely breakfast in bed with the princess, but the subsequent visit to her chambers satisfied me beyond my expectations. Until then, her presence here seemed temporary, like water that might slip from between my fingers. But seeing her so frustrated, so defiant and yet unable to leave, reassured me that no one can remove her from my grasp.

Not even herself.

My chest rumbles with pleasure.

"Soren."

Reluctantly, I bring my attention back to Rally. "What?"

"You cannot say such things to a woman."

"What things?"

"For stars' sake," he grumbles. "Did you listen to nothing Marta said?"

"I listened to everything your wife said," I answer, affronted at the suggestion. "She was most helpful." As a human female, Marta had given me invaluable advice before bringing the princess here. "She said that above all else, a woman wants to know she is safe. She was wagging a wooden spoon at me as she said it, remember?"

Rally chuckles before sobering once more. "I do."

"How much safer can the princess be than she is now?"

Princess Serah mentioned the archers herself, and she must have seen the guards in the corridor. Little does she know, even the servants' entrances are guarded.

The corner of my mouth creeps up. This is a far more promising start than the one Abely brought me.

"Soren," Rally says, his tone veering toward impatience, "that is not what Marta meant. Keeping the princess locked in her room will not make her feel safe. It will make her feel that she has no freedom."

I don't answer.

"Soren."

"What?"

"You don't honestly intend to keep her in her room all the time, do you?"

"Of course not." We pass another guard, who bows as deeply as the first. "She may leave," I say, once we pass him, "when she is with me."

Rally lays a hand on my shoulder. Normally, he would never touch me in view of others, so when he does, I stop and narrow my eyes at him. They shrink down even further as he searches my face like a physician seeking some hidden illness.

"You're prowling your territory," he says finally.

I sneer. "I am surveying the palace walls."

"I bet in about an hour, you'll have the urge to curl up in that absurd pile of pillows you keep on your bed."

My lip rises. "Perhaps I'd like a nap."

"And likely a few jewels to examine afterward."

I show him my teeth. "You go too far—"

"Soren, there are flames in your eyes."

My mouth clamps shut on the reprimand. With a casual turn of my heel, I put the palace at my back and face the city. "Tell me when they're gone."

Rally moves to stand a half pace ahead of me. I breathe, and he watches for the flames to fade.

"Gone," he says on my third exhalation.

My eyes remain on the city, on its neat shops and sturdy homes. "I gave you a difficult task, watching over your king."

"Yes," my friend says.

"If you ever wish to be relieved of it, all you need do is ask."

He snorts. "And be forced to lick your boots like everyone else? I think not."

Now that I've regained control, I easily repress the smirk his response provokes. Rally alone is allowed to speak to me as he pleases, because Rally alone is tasked with ensuring my first form doesn't emerge unless called upon. It's imperative my subjects know I hold absolute control over both forms—the man and the beast. Slip-ups cannot be tolerated.

"We knew this could happen when the princess arrived," Rally says as if reading my mind. He squints up at the sky. "A dragon with a mate—"

"Is a dangerous dragon," I finish. Every fledgling learns the line by rote. It reminds us all to give fresh couples space. If the princess and I were following dragon tradition, we would retreat to the desert for the courtship period, returning only once the more primitive urges, like hoarding, abated.

But a king cannot retreat.

"Thank you, Rally," I say as the dragon within recedes.

"Of course, Your Majesty." He pauses. "Are you going to let her out now?"

I work myself through another round of breathing before answering. "I will consider it."

We turn at the sound of anxious footsteps pelting the stone walkway. A youth, red-faced and panting, is sprinting toward us.

"That doesn't look promising," Rally says.

"Mm."

The boy arrives in a state of near collapse. He manages to bow, but when he rises to deliver the message he's been sent with, all color leaves his face. Rally and I exchange a knowing look.

"Easy, lad," Rally says, his mouth quivering as he steadies the boy.

"Speak," I say. "I will not be angry."

Not at him, anyway. His attire marks him as a simple errand boy; whatever message he brings won't be urgent, but the sender anticipated my frustration at the very least. Hence, the boy to bear the brunt, poor lad.

"Your Majesty," the boy says, flopping into a second bow. It's like he lost all his bones on the way. "I was sent...the princess..."

I stiffen. "What of the princess?"

Rally claps the boy on the back as he does some more sputtering. "Out with it."

"She's sending for pianos," the boy says, "and, well, peacocks—"

"Peacocks?" I repeat.

He bobs his head. "Yes. Oiken sent me."

My brows lower. "Oiken understands the princess is to be brought whatever she desires, yes?" My majordomo is not usually prone to error.

Somehow, the boy pales further. "Yes, yes of course, Your Majesty." He glances back and forth, wringing his hands, wetting his lips. "It's just that Oiken says the room can't fit the camel Princess Serah requested, so he isn't sure what to..." His voice dwindles away.

I allow myself a single exhalation before striding for the nearest stairwell with Rally tight on my heels.

My encounter with the king leaves me reeling. Reeling and outraged.

After he left, I retreated to my bedchamber and stormed about in a manner I haven't since, well, ever, because I had no need to storm about before meeting a certain king.

How dare he make me lose control like that. And to simply watch as I siphoned those flowers dry instead of saying anything!

"Water drawing is a gift," Mother would say, *"but an undisciplined drawer is dangerous."*

I have trained hard not to be dangerous. If the king knew what such a gift is capable of...

I press the heels of my hands against my eyes. I all but yelled the peril at him.

That's the greater source of my anger—that I revealed too much, that the control lost was my own doing, not his.

That, and the ridiculous way heat soars to my cheeks when I think of him lifting my chin. I've not even been here a full day. Doesn't he know it's improper for him to touch me as if I'm already his?

"Wholly unacceptable," I mutter.

My pacing has slowed, and I move fast to correct that. Better to be angry than dwell on impropriety.

Smoothing back my hair, I return my thoughts to the original offense. Does the king think because I am lesser royalty he can keep me in these rooms? I was prepared to sacrifice for my people, to marry a man donning horns and few feelings.

I was not prepared to be held hostage in my own rooms.

I throw myself onto the bed and lie there staring at the wall. A servant must have removed the king's breakfast tray. The idea of people I don't know coming and going unseen unsettles me a bit, though I know the practice is normal in large palaces. My sisters have said as much.

A long sigh of resignation slips out of me. I suppose I better call for a midday meal. Perhaps I should ask for something specific so I'm not brought another platter of chocolate. I hate to trouble the staff, though the king did say I need only ask for what I would like.

My mouth quirks. Perhaps I should ask that a banquet be brought just to make him regret his words. No, that won't do. The parlor is stuffed with all the nonsense he sent earlier. The room can hardly fit another—

An idea springs forth and latches on with all the tenacity of a fishhook. It's ridiculous, potentially petty, and has me grinning like a lunatic.

I've never been one to cause trouble, but that *was* before I met a certain dragon.

***

"Oh, yes. That pianoforte will go quite well next to the other in the bathing chamber. Thank you."

The four men wheeling the instrument through the parlor door smile.

"Yes, Your Highness. Right away."

I step back to allow them more space, and though nearly a dozen other servants are working furiously to widen the path to the bathing chamber, it's going to be a tight squeeze. This piano is larger than the last. Still, no one seems miffed. On the contrary, a fresh trio of giggling maids bearing stacks of Tirenthian history sweeps into the room and beams at me.

"Where would you like these, Princess Serah?" one of them asks.

I wave a hand to encompass the chaos, ducking once as a parrot passes overhead. "Anywhere you please."

Smiling, they move on. While I do wish to make a statement, I don't want my attempt at doing so to sour my relationship with the palace staff, but everyone seems satisfied with the reward I offered in exchange for their help.

I pause to reflect on the progress. The second piano should fill the bathing chamber to capacity. My bedchamber is coming along nicely as well. At this rate, we'll all be squeezed out in the next half hour. I press my lips together to keep from smiling.

It's difficult to stay in a room you cannot fit inside of.

Every now and then, Ty pokes his head in but makes no comment with his hands. Rally appears to be elsewhere at the moment. I wonder how long it will be until the king hears of this. A touch of nervousness steals through me at the thought.

"Princess Serah!"

My name is snapped out with all the ire of someone whose orderly life has been upended. When I lean past the doorframe, I find a red-faced majordomo marching my way.

"Oiken," I say, moving aside for a man cradling a potted cactus, "how lovely to see you again."

Oiken cuts a curt bow, his breath gusting out of him. He is a thin man, but I suspect he finds running uncouth and rarely partakes in it.

"I'm told you've asked for a camel," he says, the final word forced from clenched teeth.

"Indeed, with the stipulation that only an animal who might enjoy an excursion to my chambers be brought. I don't wish to frighten the poor thing."

"May I remind you," Oiken says, "there are stairs."

"Ah," I say, as if the thought never occurred to me. "You're very right. More peacocks should do then." With effort, I withhold the laugh that bubbles up.

Truly, I don't know what's come over me.

Oiken's mouth flattens to the point of disappearance. "*More* peacocks?"

"Yes, the first flock is enjoying a feast of goji berries on the balcony. Would you like to see them? I'm told they're having a fine time."

"This is unseemly," he hisses.

I think of replying that so is keeping a woman locked in her room, but at that very moment, all conversation ceases.

Because the floor is shaking.

The tremor travels up the soles of my feet, reverberates through my bones, then stops. As one, the servants freeze in place and glance at one another with wide eyes. One maid sinks beneath a table.

My throat tightens.

The tremor returns, nearer this time. Then again, nearer once more, like the footsteps of some enormous beast. When I gather my courage and peer out into the hallway, I see no one but Ty, who winces.

"Good day, Princess," Oiken says, and when I look to him, he spins around and strides off.

I suppose I deserve that.

The trembling continues, and though my knees are quaking, I stand my ground and await the dragon's arrival.

The parlor's newly-acquired collection of diversions rattle as the king closes in. A terrifying thought strikes me then.

Is he coming as an *actual* dragon?

The approaching footfalls certainly aren't those of a man. Will I turn and find myself looking into the eyes of a beast? Eyes framed by the scale I saw him take on earlier? I clutch onto the faint hope that if a camel can't mount the stairs, a dragon can't either.

A camel. What was I thinking? Why did I aggravate him so?

I ball my fists at my sides. I don't know, but I must face the consequences, me and me alone. I glance over the servants' pale faces.

"Please," I say, conjuring a smile, "if you'll exit through the servants' entrance, we can continue this later."

"There's no need."

I nearly leap from my skin at the sound of the king's voice. My head turns slowly toward the horned man who somehow appeared at my side without a sound. He regards the room with an even stare.

"Carry on," he says.

I've never seen such a sharp turnaround; all fear evaporates from the servants' faces as they fall back to their work. In seconds, the room takes on its previous volume.

"Good afternoon, Princess Serah," the king says in a voice pitched only for my ears.

I gulp down a swell of nerves. "Good afternoon, Your Majesty."

A taut silence falls between us despite the clamor of the room. I'm gathering the courage to break it when the king says in the driest tone ever heard, "A camel?"

A hysterical giggle burbles up, and I have to clamp my lips together to contain it. What is the matter with me?

"I thought to divert myself," I say, not sounding very convincing, "as you suggested."

I remind myself that this man, this king, did tell me he was going to keep me locked up like a stone in a box, which seems as equally unreasonable as asking that a camel to be brought to one's chambers. Still, as I watch a huddle of servants wrestle the second pianoforte through the bedroom, my conviction wanes further, even if they do look cheerful while doing it.

The king observes the spectacle without expression. "The staff's spirits seem high for those fulfilling such a daunting string of—" He pauses to watch a peacock strut by. "—requests."

I color. "I may have offered anyone who assisted me a day of repose. And cake." Lots of cake. "Everyone appeared pleased."

"Did they now?" the king asks.

Is he upset at the staff for helping me? That would be far worse than whatever ire he aims at me. All the anger I previously thought righteous suddenly seems childish, and my cheeks redden with shame. I peer up at the king through my lashes. "If you're going to be angry with anyone, please let it be me. They only did as I asked."

The bustle around me fades away as his eyes fall on mine, pinning me with the force of their stare.

"For someone untrained in our ways," he says, "you seem to ascertain our weaknesses with little difficulty."

My mouth goes dry. I offered the reward on a whim, or a hunch, really, based on the chocolate-laden breakfast and the king mentioning a desserts-only feast when I arrived. Everyone *likes* cake, but I wondered if dragons had a particular penchant for sweets. The staff's eager eyes had been answer enough.

"It was only a guess, Your Majesty," I whisper.

A clang rings out as someone drops a metal dish in the other room and it clatters across the floor. The king's gaze doesn't waver.

"Dragons are universally fond of cake," he says in something nearing a rumble. "Some might say they would do anything for it."

I don't know what possesses me to speak then. "And you, Your Majesty?"

His eyes graze my neck and the jewel there before returning to my face. "Oh, I absolutely would, Princess."

A gulp travels down my throat as this statement hangs between us. I have the distinct impression we're no longer speaking of cake, and a mortifying heat creeps over my face for provoking him.

Mercifully, he turns his attention from me to the room at large.

"Attention," he says.

The word is no louder than a normal speaking tone, yet everyone comes to a stop, their heads popping out from behind furniture and armloads of books. The king surveys the crowd with a cool air.

"Princess Serah and I," he says, "thank you for making her feel at home. Please, enjoy your repose and cake."

The servants share a single, gleeful look with one another before hurrying from the room, their chatter following them as they go. When the room is empty—of other people, at least. I fear it will take some time to empty it of all my ridiculous requests—the king and I are left to stare out over the mess I made.

The king tucks his hands behind his back. "It was certainly a creative solution, Princess."

My mouth tightens. "It was childish, and I apologize."

"No more childish than the dictate that prompted it."

I glance at him. He does look sincere, though I remind myself this is the same man who said mere hours ago I wasn't allowed to leave my room. He holds an arm out to me.

"Perhaps," he says, "you would allow me to accompany me on your tour of the palace by way of apology?"

I consider him. Of course I want out of this room. I could hardly find a place to sit even if I wanted to stay. But I've seen so many sides of this king in the brief time I've been here that I can't help hesitating. Is this the true him? A gentleman willing to apologize? Or did I see his true self when he threatened to bite Abely's head off? I suppose it's a bit ridiculous to think one might see another's true self in so short of time, but a baseline would be nice.

Especially when one is marrying a dragon.

Still, he seems to have forgiven me, and I ought to do the same. Holding grudges won't make marriage any easier, and we are to be man and wife soon. Dragon and wife.

This is for my people, I remind myself.

"That would be lovely," I say and take his arm.

24

I find myself cautiously enjoying the tour.

The king makes no more mention of cake. His manners are formal, almost stiff, but he takes obvious pride in showing me his home. The palace is a wonder of domes, minarets, and mosaics that leaves me dizzy with grandeur. Outside of Vasna, I've only visited the Sileshian palace, a great, hulking fortress built for protection, not beauty. The Tirenthian palace seems designed for both, though I do wonder how much protection could be needed when those within can transform into fire-breathing beasts.

More impressive than anything he shows me, however, is his memory. Every servant we pass, he introduces by name. I know every face at home, but Vasna's palace and staff is minuscule in comparison to Tirenth's.

"Greetings, Isaak," the king says as we come alongside an older man pushing a wheelbarrow beside the covered walkway we stroll. "Are you in need of assistance?"

The man pushes his hat back and glances up. His hair is white but his eyes bright and smiling. "Ah, not today, Your Majesty. These old wings still have some life in them."

He spots me, and the bright eyes widen. Dropping the wheelbarrow handles, he tugs his hat off. "The Water Bringer," he breathes, dropping to a knee.

I startle at both the title and his reverence, but the king only says, "Indeed. This is Princess Serah of Vasna."

The man lifts his shining gaze to me. "An honor, Your Highness. Truly."

"Likewise," I say, curtsying to the man who then looks apt to weep.

After helping the man up, the king guides me onward.

"Who was that?" I ask softly as we walk.

"Isaak, the chief gardener."

A quick look behind shows me the man, hat clutched to his chest, still standing where we left him.

"Older dragons," the king says as I turn back, "remember older days. They knew Tirenth when she was only sand and a few skinny palm trees on the ocean's edge. They remember a time before canals and cisterns, Princess. They remember drought."

It's the most I've heard him speak at one time, and I take care to absorb his words. Doing so also distracts me from the feel of his bicep beneath my hand, a sensation I've been pointedly ignoring since we started out. "When was the last drought?"

"Now."

I clear my throat to cover my shock. "Now?"

"Yes. The cisterns will run dry in two weeks."

He says this with an ease that has me staring at him.

"But," he says, his eyes trained forward, "you're here now, so there's no need to worry."

I'm certain my mouth would fall open if not for all my tutors' harping on composure. He expects me to end a drought? I swallow. "Water can be fickle, Your Majesty." Fickle is putting it delicately. There are a dozen factors involved—the amount of water present, how deep it is, how far away. "It could take some time."

"I have faith in you."

A fine sweat breaks out over my skin. What if there's no water to draw? Or what if the water I find is so far it takes months to draw near the city? What then?

Perform for me, Serah, and I'll give you anything you want.

Is this what he meant? Perform by ending the drought? And if I can't, does he plan on sending me home? Recalling Vasna's debts?

Seemingly out of nowhere, a blistering wind sweeps over us, pelting me with sand. Whether from instinct or surprise, I draw nearer to the king. The wind is fierce, and yet I hear a sharp intake of breath; I feel his arm stiffen beneath my hand.

"A scorcher," he shouts over the gale.

"A what?"

The king shakes his head and hurries our pace. He tucks me in tighter as the wind strengthens and I'm forced to shield my eyes. When I blink them open, we're shielded from the wind in a stone alcove fringed in flowering vines.

"A scorcher," the king says, his voice sharp as he guides me to a recessed bench carved into the wall. "That's what the wind is called. They come hard and fast off the desert."

I release his arm and sit, puzzled by his harsh tone. Did I do something to upset him? "Ah, I see. Are they common, these winds?"

When there's no answer, I sneak a glance up at him. The lines of his face are rigid, his jaw tight. His chin quivers as if restraining himself from speaking.

He looks *livid*.

Alarm courses through me. What did I say? Retracing my words, I can find nothing offensive. Is he angry I didn't sound more confident in my ability to end the drought? Should I not have moved so close to him when we could have been seen? Surely not. He held my hand in front of his subjects, in front of the wyverns even. He openly slept in my chambers for stars' sake! And yet he stands here as if frozen by rage, every inch of him but his flared nostrils still.

I pretend not to notice his face lift to sniff at the air, his breaths quicken when he does. In truth, I'm wondering once again whether he's fighting the urge to make a meal out of me. I glance about in hopes another servant is nearby, but we're alone.

"Well," I say, rising to my feet, "it sounds as if the wind has died down. These scorchers must pass quickly."

I sidle over a couple of steps, my back grazing the stone wall. The king doesn't move.

Think, Serah. Think. All I can think to do is run, but though my gown isn't restrictive, I doubt I can outpace him in it. Perhaps if I kick him first? That can hardly be good for diplomacy...

"I can't take this," he snarls.

I gasp as he whirls toward me, plants both hands on either side of the wall behind my head, and leans in, eyes wild.

"Princess, I must ask you something. *Now.*"

25

Ask me something? My heart is in my throat, and any words I might be able to force past it seem caught somewhere between my mind and my mouth.

The king's eyes bore into my own as he awaits an answer, yet I realize he hasn't even asked anything. He simply pinned me here like a barbarian.

Somehow, I swallow and manage a few breathy words. "Yes, Your Majesty?"

What could he possibly want to ask me so badly? And why does he continue to look so angry?

"Why..." His teeth grind against one another as he forms the words. "*Why do you smell like that?*"

All the breath rushes out of my lungs. Surely, I heard him wrong. "Pardon?" I squeak.

He leans in, his nose hovering over the skin of my neck. A shiver rushes over me as he inhales and releases the breath with a long, low growl. "Why," he repeats, "do you smell like that?"

"Like what, Your Majesty?"

"Like a cake," he bursts out, pushing off the wall and away from me. Dumbfounded, I watch as he begins some sort of breathing exercise, inhaling and exhaling with the lifting and lowering of his arms to his chest.

"Is it a perfume?" He grinds out. "If it is, you must—I need you to stop wearing it."

"The maids may have perfumed my hair," I stammer.

He shakes his head. "It isn't your hair. It's your skin."

My cheeks are instantly aflame. It's as I feared in the carriage. He *does* smell my sweat. I don't see what else I can do but speak my suspicion aloud. "I—I'm sweating, Sire."

"Then your sweat smells like cake," he snaps.

I doubt that, but even if it did, why does he seem so angry about it? Did he not say he liked cake?

"I apologize for offending you," I say, though in truth I'm beginning to feel a bit offended myself. What kind of man badgers a woman over sweating?

A draconic one, I suppose.

The king pinches the bridge of his nose between two fingers. "You did not offend." With a sigh, he drops his hand. "Nothing about you offends."

I simply stare at him, unable to make sense of any of this. "Do dragons not sweat?"

"No," he says, staring off as if facing some terrible foe. I take the opportunity to smooth out my gown. Tongues will certainly wag if I emerge from here with a red face *and* rumpled clothing.

My hands pause.

Isn't that what we want?

Biting my lip, I consider the ploy an instant longer before seizing handfuls of my gown and crumpling them in my fists.

"What are you doing?" the king asks in bewilderment.

"Reinforcing the idea we're fated flames." Though I feel my cheeks reddening further, I keep at it, even tugging a lock of hair from the unassailable updo Hiln made atop my head.

Mother would be horrified. Likely, my sisters, too. But none of them are here, and there are barely four weeks until the wedding. I need to lock in my position, especially in light of the king's volatile ways. If his subjects believe I belong here, perhaps that will carry some weight should their ruler want to send me home for sweating or whatever the day's misdeed might be.

The ruse complete, I force myself to look at the king.

To my untold shock, his face is even redder than mine.

We stare at one another with wide eyes until suddenly, with a grunt, he marches to my side, seizes my hand, and starts hauling me down the walkway.

"Where are we going?" I ask.

"To the kitchens."

"For the evening meal?"

"For cake."

***

The kitchen we arrive in, though larger than any I've seen, is in the same state as any other—a great bustle of noise, smells, and steam. There's something comforting about the familiarity, and even more so when the scent of warm sugar is added to it.

The head baker greets us with genuine delight, ushering us over to a small table in the corner of the kitchen. A clean cloth is tossed over it, and in moments, the entire surface is piled high with cakes, pastries, and custards, each dessert more beautiful than the last.

The king falls immediately upon the platter of small, glistening cakes that are set in front of him while I stare down at the perfect sphere of ruby red something presented to me.

"It's flavored with pomegranate juice," the king says through a mouthful of cake. "Try it."

"It's so pretty," I say, admiring the unfamiliar texture. "May I ask what it is?"

The corner of his lip creeps up. "Just try it."

His gaze tracks my hand as I bring the spoon to my lips.

"It's cold," I gasp, my eyes swelling with delight.

"It's a sorbet."

"Sorbet," I repeat, admiring it anew. "Am I meant to eat this with it?" I point my spoon at a delicate sprig of mint.

"No, it's garnish."

"Ah."

Silence falls between us as we eat, though it's not an uncomfortable one. It's almost companionable. The kitchen staff sneaks furtive glances at us, but for the most part, they bustle about as if a king in the kitchen is an everyday occurrence. By the speed at which the spread before us was brought, I wouldn't doubt it is.

How my sisters would love this, I think as I reach the bottom of my dish. I've never seen such delicacies, not even at weddings. Most of my people will never see such at all.

Most of my people are struggling to keep their families fed, and yet they always keep smiles on their faces. Suddenly, the spoon in my hand feels like a leaden weight heaped high with guilt.

"What's the matter?" the king asks, startling me from my thoughts.

"Oh, nothing, Your Majesty." Smiling, I glance about the table. "Which of these do you recommend I try next?"

His chewing slows as he observes me. "I sense you are not being truthful, Princess."

A denial rises to my lips, but before I can give voice to it, he adds, "Forgive me if I'm mistaken."

The preemptive apology softens me more than I wish, though I can't say why. I look away. "You are not mistaken, sire."

He remains quiet, his eyes fixed on my face when I wish he would look elsewhere. I'm not made for lies, and I know this. I don't *like* lying. Still, I don't want to tell him more either. Doing so would only expose weakness, which mother would scold me soundly for.

"It has been a difficult few years for my people," I say finally, lifting my chin. "I think often of them." There. That's simple enough.

The king regards me with a level gaze. "And you feel guilty for indulging when they cannot."

The astute analysis takes me aback. I don't know what I expected, but it wasn't that. "Yes," I say.

"You care deeply for them."

Faces flash before my mind's eye—old ones, young ones, those of fishermen, and farmers, those of my sisters and mother, each of them precious to me before and even more so now that they're far away.

"I do," I say, and to my horror, I feel tears springing to my eyes even as the king watches.

What is the matter with me? I cannot cry here in front of everyone! A kitchen girl stirring the contents of the bowl is glancing my way right now. "My apologies, sire. Perhaps we could speak of something else." I swipe at my treacherous eyes. "I don't wish for anyone to think something is wrong between us."

He pats his mouth with a napkin and rises. "Then let us retire," he says, holding a hand out to me.

I blink at him. "It isn't even sunset."

He shrugs. "The staff won't expect to see us often out of the bedchamber anyway."

I'd normally be scandalized by his insinuation, but what can I say? Crumpling my skirt and mussing my hair as I did? In truth, I am tired in body and spirit and retiring early sounds marvelous. Perhaps I can take one of the Tirenthian history tomes brought earlier with me to bed and lose myself in some reading.

Taking the dragon's hand, I let him lead me through a side door and back into the open air.

***

The king maintains a slow pace so that by the time we reach the building where my chambers are, the sun is setting, the sky lit by all the fiery hues of a freshly-lit torch.

If I were at home, I'd be settling my goats in their stall for the night, scratching each of their heads between their horns. Thankfully, the walk calmed me enough that I can think of them without more tears. I do hope Selena is making sure they stay milked on time. Stella gets cranky if not.

I keep hold of the king's arm as he escorts me through the main doors and up the marble steps.

"I'll have your evening meal sent here," he says.

"Thank you," I answer, touched and surprised by his thoughtfulness. When I think back on our afternoon spent together, I find it overall pleasant. Well, other than his strange reaction to my scent. Yet another blush creeps up my neck at the thought of him pinning me in place, his eyes somehow both savage and desperate. I didn't like it, of course. No self-respecting lady would.

No, I tell myself sternly, *I didn't like it all.*

I turn my thoughts elsewhere as we move down the hallway. Two silent guards stand on either side of the first door, and here is where the king stops. I glance down the hallway at my own door, currently flanked by double guards as well.

"My apologies, Your Majesty, but my door is the next," I say.

The king takes hold of the handle. "I know."

His eyes lock onto mine and hold me there. He leans in. He's near enough for me to feel the heat of his skin.

"Tonight," he says, "you stay with me."

26

I do my best to blush prettily in front of the guards as the king gazes down at me, but I do believe I'm going to faint right here in this hallway.

Stay with *him*? What does he mean?

Not taking his eyes off me, the king says to one of the guards, "Have Princess Serah's evening meal sent to my chambers."

The smile in the guard's voice makes me wish I would faint. "With pleasure, Your Majesty," he says, and bowing, he's off.

I barely restrain myself from gasping aloud as the king splays his hand across the small of my back and guides me inside. As soon as the door clicks shut behind us, he drops the hand, leaving the skin there oddly chilled. I take a tremulous breath as he moves a step away.

"You might have warned me," I say, striving for a dignified tone.

The king tilts his head at me, his expression indiscernible. "I assumed you knew."

"Knew what?"

"That you would stay here."

I gape at him, too shocked to do any more blushing. "Why in all the stars' names would you think that?"

"Where in your chambers did you intend to sleep, Princess?"

Oh. Somehow, I'd forgotten the mess I'd left in my rooms. The king watches the realization play out across my face and says, "Perhaps we could convince the peacocks to share some space with you."

Sharp words rise to my tongue, but when I see his mouth twitch, I realize he's made a joke, one meant to put me at ease. A small smile touches my own lips.

"Do you really think they're still there?" I ask.

"No. They will have left by the balcony by now."

"Unless they can't make their way past the pianos."

He lets out a chuckle, a sound deep and low enough to reverberate through my chest as well. "I'll have it all removed tomorrow," he says, "so you can be restored to your own rooms."

"Thank you."

"And I will be sure your things have been delivered."

My smile falters, but I recover it before he notices. "Thank you, Your Majesty."

He inclines his head and moves deeper into the room, giving me the first chance to look around. The wall sconces have already been lit, and yet the space is a dark, brooding one filled with shadows cast by imposing furniture, the largest of which is a curtained, four-poster bed nearly buried in crimson and gold brocade pillows, all of them swathed in silk and velvet. One particularly dark corner of the room is stacked to the ceiling with what appears to be wooden chests.

In short, it's exactly what one would expect the room of a dragon king to be. It even smells faintly of smoke, though it's overlaid with the stronger scents of leather and sandalwood.

I look back to the king to see he's already shrugged out of his armored coat and is working at the shirt beneath. He lifts a brow as he catches me looking.

"Did you want to bathe first?" he asks. "I assumed you wanted to wait for your meal."

Bathe?

Oh, stars.

"I do," I say. "Wish to wait for my meal, that is. I will wait here." I fairly leap to a thick-legged table tucked in the corner. "Right here."

His gaze lingers on me a moment longer before he turns toward a door I assume leads to the bathing chamber.

"Wait," I say, a thought only just now occurring. "Are you not hungry?" He only requested a meal for me, not one for himself.

He glances back. "I ate seventeen cakes."

"*Seventeen?*" I stare at him. I ate a single sorbet in that time!

"I am a dragon, Princess."

"Of course."

He disappears into the bathing chamber, and I begin trying to collect my thoughts.

Him staying in my chambers was scandalous enough, but to be brought to his so openly, to have his hand upon me in front of the guards...I press the back of my hands to my cheeks in a futile attempt to cool them.

It's for the best, I tell myself. News that I'm staying here will spread quickly through the staff, and that will only help drive home this fated flames business. The king said it was the only way his subjects would accept a human ruler, so this is good. Preferable, even. I sit at the table, my eyes fixed on the bathing chamber door.

Did he take any clothing in with him? I didn't see any. What if he intends to come out in a towel?

What if he intends to wear nothing at all?

A knock at the servant's door sends me flying to my feet. A meal will be a welcome distraction. When I open the door, I'm surprised and delighted to see a face I recognize.

"Cora," I say, "how lovely to see you again."

Beaming, the girl curtsies. "Same to you, Your Highness."

I stand aside so she can bring the tray in. "Did you have a good tour of the palace?" she asks, but no sooner have the words left her mouth than she winces. "My apologies, ma'am."

"For what?"

"For asking," she says, eyes on the dishes she's now arranging on the table. "Hiln says I talk too much to the nobles. I don't mean to. I was just raised friendly is all. I forget myself."

"Hiln is entitled to her own opinion," I say, settling into a chair, "but your friendliness is most welcome here."

A ghost of a smile plays over her lips. "Thank you, Your Majesty. I'll keep that in mind."

Satisfied, I glance over the spread before me as Cora fills a glass with a sweet-smelling wine.

"I don't think I can eat half of this," I say under my breath.

Cora chuckles. "That's what I said, but Hiln insisted, and I dare not fight her."

"She does seem formidable."

A quiet laugh that could pass for a cough is the only response. "Is there anything else I can do for you, Your Majesty?"

"Might you check on my cat friend?"

Her eyes lift, and glancing behind me, she points toward the bed. To my shock, when I turn to look, he's now lounging there amongst the pillows. "How does he do that?"

Cora shrugs. "He's a cat. You'll have to name him soon, you know."

"Indeed."

Taking up her tray, she says, "Is there anything else you'd like?"

"Might you loosen my gown before you go?" I glance toward the bathing chamber, which is still silent. "So that no one else has to come later?"

Though no one has said so, I suspect Hiln is my actual ladies' maid, and that such a thing is her job. At home, I rarely wore gowns that required assistance, but the one I was put in this morning will be a challenge to remove without ripping.

Cora folds her lips together. "Begging your pardon, ma'am, but Hiln had thoughts on that as well." Darting her own glance toward the bathing chamber, she leans near and in a hushed tone, says, "She was of the idea males like to do that sort of work themselves."

She and I both color up to our eyebrows.

"Oh," I say.

"Mm," she says.

And we both color some more, if that's even possible.

"Well—" Cora clears her throat. "If you're not needing anything else, I'll be off." Curtsying once more, she scuttles for the door.

"Thank you, Cora," I call after her.

She bobs a curtsy once more. Hesitates.

"Might I say one thing more, Your Highness?"

"Of course." I fortify myself for more of Hiln's disconcerting advice, but the way Cora's eyes brighten suggest the words to come are her own.

"The staff," she says, "we're real glad you're here. We've waited a long time for a queen. His Majesty has waited a long time." She hugs the tray to herself. "There'll be some who are unkind because, well, they're not used to humans, and they had their own ideas about who the king should marry, but I hope you'll like Tirenth anyway. Truly, I do."

Before I can respond—or even think how to—the bathing chamber door creaks opens and Cora bolts from the room.

Leaving me to face the king as he stalks out in a cloud of steam.

27

First, I thank the Maker of Stars that he's clothed.

Second, I wonder why it feels as if my heart has suddenly migrated to my throat.

I've already seen him shirtless—an image I banish as quickly as possible from my mind—so I can't imagine why a loose shirt and trousers should elicit such a response, but here I am, breathless and staring at the way the thin fabric clings to his still-damp skin as he tousles his hair with a towel, the dark horns gleaming in between.

"I hope I didn't keep you waiting, Princess," he says, seemingly oblivious to my gawking at him. "Was the meal to your satisfaction?"

The meal? *The meal.* I dive into my food with all the enthusiasm of someone who hasn't eaten in days.

"Oh, yes," I say before cramming in another bite. "Delicious."

He stays where he is a moment more before moving to the bed. When the rustle of blankets hits my ears, I nearly leap from the chair.

"I'll take my bath now," I say, and wiping my mouth, I dart toward the bathing chamber.

"Would you like me to call someone to help with your gown?"

I whirl around. "What?"

Contrary to what I thought, it isn't the blankets he's adjusting; it's the mountain of pillows on his bed. He seems to be arranging a number of them into a pallet on the floor.

"Your gown," he says, not looking up from his task. "Don't you need help to—" He studies the pillow in his hands with immense interest, finally clearing his throat to finish with, "to remove it?"

I tuck my hands behind my back to hide how I'm twisting them together. How to tell him? "I did try asking, Your Majesty."

His head jerks up. "Did someone refuse you?"

A spark lights in his eyes, and panic has me saying, "No, of course not. They seemed to be under the impression you would help me, and I didn't correct them considering this fated flames business..."

My words dwindle off as he continues staring at me. The only reaction he offers is a prolonged blink before returning to his pillow arranging.

"Do you wish for me to help?" he asks.

Of course not, is on the tip of my tongue. Appearances for the sake of his court is one thing. Actually asking him to assist in something so intimate is quite another.

And yet what if I tear the dress trying to loosen it on my own? The staff may think me ungrateful, or they may wonder why the king didn't help me like they assumed he would.

No, they'll likely assume he tore it himself in a fit of passion, which would be far more mortifying.

Worse than all, though: What if he takes my request as an invitation? I know what is expected of me after the ceremony, of course, and I'm willing to fulfill my duties, but...

"Princess?"

I startle from my trance. How long have I stood here staring at him?

"I'm not sure," I answer finally, because despite years of tutelage, I can't think of anything more clever to say.

The king straightens slowly, his expression opaque. Have I offended him? I suppose it's not every day that someone questions his help. Kings are used to hearing *yes*.

"Many have reason to fear me, Princess," he says at last.

I swallow as he meets my eye with deliberate calm.

"My queen never will."

With that said, he picks up another pillow and studies the floor for the proper placement.

Again, an intelligent response eludes me. I stand there, silent and perplexed.

If my parents' marriage taught me anything, it was that a man of unpredictable moods can always turn on the one who tries loving him best, and he likely will. So why am I tempted to believe this dragon king who has shown me half a dozen different sides of himself already?

Mother would tell me not to be foolish. My sisters would say the same, all of them but Selena, who claims she'll only marry someone who's madly (*wretchedly* I believe was the exact word) in love with her. Young as she is, she would understand this hope in my heart that I'm trying in vain to tamp down.

It can't be wrong to hope for something more, can it? Something better than an indifferent alliance?

I take a hesitant step closer.

"Then I would be most grateful for your assistance," I say.

The king's movements slow. He rises like a man who stumbled on a frightened animal he doesn't wish to spook, approaching on silent feet. Now he stands in front of me, his face perfectly impassive.

"Turn around," he says.

I do so, clutching my hands in front of me. When his touch comes, there's only a swift untying of the lacing ribbon at my back, his fingertips feathering over my skin but never lingering. Unwillingly, a shiver trembles up my spine. The fingers pause before continuing.

"Done," he says, short and gruff as he thuds his way back to his pile of pillows. "You'll find everything you need for your bath in the cabinets."

I whisper a breathy *thank you* and dash to the bathing chamber.

Inside, and with the door latched, I lean against the wood and try to understand this regret welling up in me. What did I expect? For him to fall all over himself? Confess his undying love? Ridiculous. Sighing, I take in the space in front of me.

Unsurprisingly, the bathing chamber is lavish, with ornately-tiled surfaces and a great, circular tub at the center of the room. Two spigots feed directly into the tub, one hot and one cold, an untold luxury for someone whose mother made sure she wasn't above hauling her own heated water to a wooden tub.

Beneath a latticework window, I find the cabinets the king spoke of, and upon opening one, I nearly squeal. Rows of soaps, oils, perfumes, and herbs await me, and this time, I get to choose.

I'm about to have the best bath of my *life*.

While the tub fills, I make my selections– a bit of rose-water, a handful of lavender, and another of chamomile. Finally, I slip off my loosened dress and drop into the steaming water with a soft exhale.

I've always felt at home in the water, and tonight is no different. My muscles instantly loosen; my worries quiet. With the door locked and my mind at ease, I rest my head on the back of the tub, fully relaxed.

In time, I begin twirling a single finger, coaxing the water to circle me in little eddies. It's the first time I've used my power like this since leaving Vasna, and the feeling is welcoming, like a friend's embrace after a long absence. I continue playing with the water till it froths and bubbles around me, and then I draw in a great breath and sink beneath the surface.

At home, my sisters and I sometimes spent hours diving for pearls, carefully prying open oysters and competing for the largest treasure. I never won, but I gained plenty of experience holding my breath. I fall easily into the habit of pursing my lips and releasing a bubble every now and then as time drifts away from me, the only sounds the water's churning and my heartbeat in my ears as I soak up the drowsy peace. If only I had gills like the fabled merpeople, I could fall asleep here.

A shadow falls over me.

My eyes ease open, and I barely have time to register the murky figure above before a hand is in my hair, dragging me to the surface.

28

I come up from the water sputtering with fright and out-rage.

"Let go," I cry, and though the hand in my hair imme-diately releases me, I lift my own hand in a backhanded motion and begin flinging the bath water in whip-like tendrils at my attacker.

"Ow!"

"Get out," I scream, continuing the barrage with one hand while swiping my eyes with the other. "Get out!"

My attacker shields his face with an arm and stum-bles back. I can't hear what he—for the voice is decidedly male—is saying over the water's lashing, or see his face between my blows, but I'll make sure whoever it is regrets ambushing a water drawer in a tub.

"Princ—," the man splutters, "stop—I didn't mean—*argh*!"

I gasp as a spout of crimson flame arcs out and my water whips dissipate in a hiss of steam.

Leaving a panting and very wet king staring back at me. Our eyes widen on one another.

"Your Majesty," I say, deference overtaking me in the in-stant before I remember he's invading *my* privacy. "What are you doing here?" I demand.

He scrubs at his face like an angry cat.

"You were in here so long," he says, flinging water onto the floor, "and I called, and I knocked. When you didn't answer, I assumed you were in danger."

In danger of what? Drowning in a tub? "I simply did not hear you. My head was under the water."

"As I saw." He scowls at me. "What were you doing?"

"I was attempting to relax, Your Majesty."

"Relax? How can that possibly be relaxing?"

"Well, I simply hold my breath, and—"

"Hold your breath?" He eyes me with suspicion. "I knocked for some time. How long can you hold your breath like that?"

I toss a hand up in aggravation. "A couple of minutes? I don't know. I haven't counted in some time."

"A couple of minutes?" He gapes at me. "Why would anyone want to spend a couple of minutes underwater?"

"It's soothing." I look him up and down. "That is when one is not being yanked about by their hair."

His irritation fizzles out like a doused fire. He glances aside, fixing his gaze on the nearest wall. "I apologize, Princess. I would not have touched you in so coarse a manner had I known where else to take hold."

Fresh alarm sends heat racing up my face as the full implication of his words strikes me.

He stood over me, and so he saw me completely and utterly naked.

"As it was," the king continues, "the light is dim, and the water obscured your figure." His jaw works a moment. "I thought it unwise to reach for you...unguided, even considering my concerns."

A thread of relief trickles through me. Perhaps he didn't see. He clears his throat.

"Did I hurt you?"

I glance up at these quieter words from him. "No," I say. Or rather no more than Hiln did wrenching my hair into this arrangement. It's been tugging at my scalp all day. "Did...did I hurt you?"

"No." Still averting his eyes, he cuts a quick bow. "I apologize again, Princess. I'll leave you now."

He turns on his heel and stalks out the door, or rather, the opening in the wall.

The door has been ripped away, as if by the jaws of a great beast.

I finish washing, one eye on the mangled doorway all the while.

***

I emerge sometime later clutching my bundled dress in front of me and trying in vain to avoid the king's notice.

I fail, of course.

He waits in a dark, hulking chair and, to my surprise, he appears to be reading a book. As I creep toward the pillow pallet, his eyes rise over the pages, and when they fall on me, he freezes in place.

"I apologize," I murmur as he takes in my attire. "I didn't bring anything else."

In all my fretting over sharing his chambers, I forgot to ask for a change of clothing. Remembering that he didn't take anything with him into the bathing chamber, I opened every cabinet and found a pile of outfits similar to his, and discovering the pants to be far too large, that left me the option of swathing myself in towels or wearing a lone shirt. So here I stand in one of the king's shirts and nothing else.

"We seem to be doing a lot of apologizing this evening," the king says, his eyes locked onto mine.

"Indeed."

"You, however, owe me none, Princess. Whatever is mine is yours."

"Thank you, Your Majesty."

Ducking my head, I bolt my way to the pillow pallet. The faster I can hide myself the better. To my dismay, the pallet appears to have no blankets, only pillows. I bite my lip. I suppose I could take a blanket from the bed, though a lifetime of living with sisters has taught me that people can be particular about their bedding. Mirelle might start a war over someone touching her linens.

"Do you need something?"

I wince at the question. Why can't he focus on his book? Still clinging to my dress, I turn to face him.

"Might there be another blanket about?" I ask in as dignified a manner as possible.

The king lowers the book to his lap. "Are there not enough on the bed? I can call for more."

"Oh, no, that won't be necessary." The idea of anyone else seeing me like this is too much for an evening already fraught with embarrassment. No, I'll simply bury myself in pillows and pray sleep comes quickly. I ease down on the largest one I can find—a behemoth of crimson silk—and begin piling smaller ones around me.

"What are you doing?"

I glance up at his tone. He sounds mystified when the answer is obvious. "I'm arranging my bed, Your Majesty."

"Arranging your...?" He stares at me, aghast. I start as the book slams shut with a thump. "You're not sleeping *there*," he says, pronouncing the last word as if he's speaking of a dung heap.

I blink at him. "Pardon?"

He shoots to his feet, all indignation. "My future queen sleep on the *floor*?" He looks appalled. "Never."

"But, this is your room..." In my room was different. Here, I assumed he would sleep in his own bed.

He storms over, seizes the pillow in my hands, and tosses it over his shoulder. "Did you not hear me? What's mine is yours."

With how outraged he looks, I'm surprised to find myself near laughing. "Would that not also apply to the pillows then?"

His brows knit together. "No, not tonight. You can reclaim them again tomorrow." He holds a hand out to me.

Stifling a smile, I take it and let him draw me to my feet. All humor fades as his eyes meet mine and I once again become aware of how little I'm wearing. My cheeks and chest and all the rest of me feel flushed, like I'm suffering from some euphoric fever. When I pull away, the king releases me without lingering, and again I feel that absurd regret as I scramble into the bed and under the covers.

I listen as the king moves about the room, snuffing the sconces first and opening one of the many chests stacked in that shadowed corner next. I wonder what he keeps in them. Surely any gold, or jewels, or the like would be kept in a royal vault, wouldn't they?

Finally, I hear him settle amongst the pillows beside the bed. A long, distinctly uncomfortable silence, the kind that only brews in the darkness when something might be said but nothing is, ensues. The king draws in a long breath.

"So you can wield water like a weapon," he says.

"So you can do so with fire," I reply.

The words seem fit for the dark. I don't think either of us wanted to admit how surprised we were in that moment. Stories said dragons breathed fire, but none mentioned the same for their human forms. I doubt the king was any better prepared to be flogged by water.

Somehow, the silence feels less oppressive afterwards. I reach out for my cat friend, but he seems to have moved on from earlier. I even feel around with my feet to see if he's at the bottom of the bed. I wish he were here to hold. I wrap my arms around a pillow and pull it close.

Sleep doesn't come. What does are Cora's words from earlier.

There'll be some who are unkind because, well, they're not used to humans, and they had their own ideas about who the king should marry...

The speech was meant kindly, of that I'm sure. Still, as the minutes drag by, I can't help fixating on "their own ideas about who the king should marry." Like who?

I'm not a fool; the Dragon King may not be human, but that doesn't mean every ruler on the continent wasn't fighting to send their daughters to him. An alliance with Tirenth is a powerful one indeed. No one would dare harass the country allied with the dragon kingdom.

Well, that allied country will soon be Vasna, so what does it matter what people think? It doesn't. I roll to my other side.

"Why aren't you asleep?" the king asks after I shift positions yet again.

"I apologize."

He sighs. "You don't need to apologize." He pauses as if considering something. "You're accustomed to sleeping alone, as am I. We will grow used to one another."

I'm quiet at this. Mother said all kings keep mistresses and to prepare myself for that. Does his comment mean he doesn't have them? Perhaps he only sends them away after the deed is done. The thought makes me grimace, and though the king can be, well, boorish at times, I can't quite imagine him doing something so distasteful. Maybe I'm being idealistic, fancying him someone he isn't to suit myself. Or maybe...

Maybe this king is different.

"Until yesterday, I'd never slept in a room with a man," I say in response.

"It may comfort you to remember that I'm not one."

I clap my hand over a spurt of laughter.

"Was that humorous?" he asks.

"Yes."

"I'm glad."

I smile in the dark, and with a final adjustment of blankets, drift off to sleep.

***

When my eyes open to morning light, I'm less surprised to sense someone beside me.

Yesterday, I'd been too shocked by the king's presence in my bed to notice how cold desert mornings can be. Now that I do notice, the frigid air against my face makes the blankets' warmth that much more delicious, and I burrow down deeper with a contented sigh.

That sigh turns into a sharp breath as the king lets out a groan and rolls over, his foot coming to rest against my own.

With my back to him, I can't tell if he's facing me or not, though what difference it makes, I don't know. What I do know is that the feel of his skin on mine feels unreasonably nice. It's a *foot* for stars' sake.

I should move. That's what a respectable woman would do, and that's what I am.

I remind myself of this a full five times before making an actual attempt. Easing the blankets back, I try extricating my legs as quietly as I can.

Just as I'm about to rise, a hand clamps onto my wrist. I whip around to find a sleepy eye glaring up at me from a nest of blankets.

"Where are you going?" the king slurs.

"I thought to get up?"

He rolls his head back and forth. "Perhaps you've forgotten," he says, "but a dragon never does."

"Forgotten?" I glance about me in confusion. "Forgotten what?"

The king narrows his already squinting eyes at me. "You owe me a debt, Princess."

29

Last night made me feel as if the king and I may someday come to understand one another Perhaps we may even be friends.

Looking at him now, scowling and going on about debts first thing in the morning, makes me think that was some fantastical dream I had.

"As I recall," I say with a sniff of distaste, "you and I entered into a mutually beneficial arrangement wherein you receive a wife who can draw water, and I—"

The king buries his face in his pillow and lets out an incoherent string of grumbling.

I lift a brow. "What?"

His head lolls my way. "I said, too many words, Princess. It's *morning*."

My mouth drops open. "You started this with all your talk of debts."

"*Debt*. Singular." He smacks his lips together. "You owe me breakfast."

For several seconds, we merely look at one another.

"Breakfast?" I say.

"Yes. You agreed to have breakfast with me yesterday, but—" He opens his mouth in a colossal yawn, giving me the impression of a forbidding cave. "We were interrupted."

I roll my lips together. *Interrupted*, is a tame way to describe yesterday morning. First, his sister, who I worried was a mistress, burst into the room, followed by Minister Abely, who very nearly lost his head.

"Indeed we were," I say diplomatically.

"I will, of course, uphold my end of the bargain as well," he says.

Tired of standing and shivering from the morning chill, I sit and gather some of the blankets to cover myself. The king keeps clinging to my wrist like a sticker burr. "I did not realize breakfast was a contractual agreement, Your Majesty."

He looks flabbergasted. "It's breakfast, Princess."

With effort, I maintain a straight face. "Of course. Might you remind me of your part in the bargain?"

At that, his fingers uncurl from my wrist. "That you'll not have to see hair or hide of me for the rest of the day."

Ah, I do remember now, and at the time, that seemed like a gift. Before I can think how to respond now, the king reaches out and tugs the bell-pull.

"Wake me when they come," he says, and cocoons himself in the blankets again.

I look at his huddled form another moment before rising and padding to the bathing chamber to relieve myself. When I finish, I stand at one of the massive mirrors within, shivering and hugging myself.

Mother told me not to get attached, for that way lies a heart never at rest. Cassandra essentially said the same, and though we rarely hear from my sister Ambril, she would likely agree, too.

Then why do I dislike the idea of not seeing him all day? I barely know him. I give myself a stern look in the glass. We spent a nice day together, and I'm craving familiarity; that's all.

Isn't it?

I run my hands down my face then continue staring into the mirror as if the answer lies there in the rumpled lines of the king's borrowed shirt.

One hand comes up to touch the sapphire at my throat. Somehow, I forgot I was wearing it. I've worn it since the king placed it there, not even thinking to remove it for my bath. How odd.

At last, I turn from the mirror and march back into the bedchamber. Mother also taught me to take calculated risks. A king with at least some attachment to me would surely make a better ally, wouldn't he?

"I'm not interested in your end of the bargain," I declare to the heap of blankets in front of me.

Once spoken, the words sound a bit ridiculous, like a child explaining why they shouldn't have to do their lessons. I'm not used to voicing my opinion uninvited. Maybe I shouldn't have said anything. Maybe he fell back asleep and didn't hear me anyway. I shift from foot to foot, the floor freezing beneath my toes.

"Then I ask it as a favor," the king says, perfectly awake.

I frown. A favor? To not have to spend the day with me? Something pinches in my chest at the request.

"Is my company that distasteful to you, Your Majesty?"

I try to keep my tone lighthearted and aloof, as if I couldn't care less. I'm not sure how well I succeed.

The king *actually* *laughs*, the sound a full-throated, hearty thing, as if I made a stupendous joke.

"No, Princess." He rolls over to face me, and his brow immediately furrows at my trembling. "What is the matter?"

"I'm cold," I say.

When he lifts the blankets for me, I join him without argument. The warmth within is divine, and for a second, I forget what we were even talking about.

I don't forget how close our half-clothed bodies are.

"Tonight is the feast celebrating your arrival," he says, and when I lift my eyes to his, he finishes with, "I must go see the wyverns."

"What? Why?"

I can see little other than his eyes and horns, and even so, I can tell he's debating with himself on how much to say.

"The peace between dragons and wyverns is tenuous at best," he says. "They claim territory in the mountains north of the desert, but right now a large party of them is gathered in a temporary camp outside of the city."

"Why so close?"

"For the same reason so many dignitaries have arrived early for the wedding. Tirenth is not usually open to guests. They have come to see the kingdom." He props himself up on one elbow. "And you."

My eyes fall. "I think you are overestimating their interest in me, sir."

"I think not."

I'm tempted to tell him that if such were the case, I would not be the only water drawer in my family's history to receive a single offer of marriage. Each of my sisters received no less than three. My grandmother, the last water drawer before me, received *nineteen*.

I don't tell him any of this because a knock at the servant's door signals breakfast, and the conversation is dropped. I smile and blush as the maids bustle about, first arranging our trays and then picking up our discarded clothing, which is bound to spur more gossip on.

"Princess," the king says as he finishes off his third pastry, "I wonder if you might do me a favor today."

Another favor? The maids continue tidying, though I know every word we say will be passed along downstairs.

"What might that be, Your Majesty?"

He picks up a chocolate-covered raspberry. "The Lady Tilanthia has requested your company today. Might you entertain her while I attend to some other matters?"

Well, this is low. His asking me while servants are about gives me little choice. If I say no to visiting with his sister, the word will spread through the palace within the hour.

"I'd love to, Your Majesty." I grace him with a vapid smile. "Will there be anything else I can do for you?"

"Yes, I wonder if you might choose my attire for this evening. I want to wear something that pleases you."

I stab at a poached egg with my fork. "Do you have a preferred color?"

"No, though perhaps something that's easily removed would suit best."

A maid audibly gasps, and I nearly choke on my egg.

"Of course," I say when I find my voice.

I don't dare say anything else, and when he dresses and returns to the bedside, I can barely meet his eyes. Taking up my hand, he bends low over it.

"Until tonight," he says.

I still as he presses his lips to my knuckles.

When he leaves, all I can think is that a king really ought to play fair.

***

Lady Tilanthia arrives in a flurry of skirts, perfume, and irresistible warmth.

"Oh, Serah," she says, embracing me as if we're old friends. "Soren told me we're to spend the afternoon together. What should we do first?"

She offers a myriad of suggestions before we settle on cards. I despise cards but can't bear to tell that to someone who looks so cheery.

"I'll teach you quandary," she says. "It's all the rage in Ilanthren."

She drags me into an adjacent room that I expect to be a misplaced parlor, but which turns out to be a small, snug library. I gaze up at the stuffed shelves stretching all the way to the ceiling. There are nearly as many books here as there are in my mother's library.

Lady Tilanthia and I settle in at a stout table and begin to play. The game is simple enough and after two rounds, I beat her at another three.

"To tell the truth, I'm terrible at this game," Lady Tilanthia laughs. "I'm always talking too much to pay attention."

I smile. "Being a good conversationalist is a far more valuable skill."

She lays down another pair of ill-fated cards with a frown. "Do you really think so?"

"I do." All her questions have been thoughtful and kind, and none of them prying.

"I've been told I talk a bit too much," she says, studying her hand with downcast eyes.

Mother told me not to get attached to my spouse. She said nothing of future siblings, and I already feel a surge of sisterly indignation for this sweet spirit.

"Perhaps whoever said so could stand to speak a little less themselves," I say, prompting a small smile from her.

She asks me of Vasna and my sisters, of my people and even my own interests. It's hard to imagine someone taking issue with her open, friendly way.

"Enough of me," I say finally. "Tell me of your own interests."

"Oh, well..." She tucks a lock of fiery hair behind her ear. "I enjoy good company."

I recognize the signal and respond accordingly with a conspiratorial smile. "Anyone in particular?"

She rolls her lip between her teeth. "Lord Lyken."

Lord Lyken? The overseer of Tirenth's western province? He has to be her senior by a decade, at least. To say I'm surprised is an understatement, but I keep my expression neutral.

"I see. He is a bit older than you, isn't he?" Yesterday, I guessed her age at fifteen or sixteen. I have a feeling the king will not approve.

A strong feeling.

"I know that," she says, "but he's funny and kind, and we both love flowers."

"Is that so?"

She nods eagerly. "That's where I met him, in the eastern gardens. He was overseeing the planting of an exquisite bed of mourning irises there."

"Really? Are they rare?"

Her eyes light up, and she launches into a discourse of surprising depth on the characteristics of the mourning iris. I guide her onto other flowers, and the subject of Lord Lyken is safely left behind.

"Is anyone in your family fond of gardening?" she asks after a while.

"My mother," I say before thinking. "She's a skilled herbalist."

"How wonderful! Who taught her?"

"I'm not sure, but do you think we should call for the midday meal?"

The remainder of the afternoon passes quicker than I expect. We eat and talk and laugh with ease. My cat friend emerges to briefly lie in my lap before flopping over in the waning sunlight cast upon the floor.

"I should go," Lady Tilanthia says. "I'm sure your maids will be here soon to dress you for the feast."

"This early?"

She giggles. "Of course. This is your first public appearance after all."

With so much else on my mind, I hadn't thought of that. Lady Tilanthia rises to straighten her copious skirts.

"Before I leave…" She grimaces. "Was everything all right with Minister Abely yesterday?"

I occupy myself with my own gown. "Well, the king allowed him to keep his head, so I suppose so."

"Soren threatened to take his *head* off?"

I glance up at her stunned tone. I thought another dragon wouldn't be surprised by his reaction, but her gaping mouth says otherwise. Maybe I was too loose with my words. "Um, perhaps? But he did not make good on his threat."

She stares at me. Then she grins.

"What?" I ask.

"You must be driving him mad for him to act that way."

My cheeks ignite. "I don't know about that."

"I do. Soren never loses control."

Now I'm the one staring. I'm just about to ask her if we're talking about the same king when there's a curt knock at the door and Hiln bursts in, her troop of maids at the ready.

"You," she says, jabbing a finger my way, "Enough talk. Time to get ready."

30

I stand in front of the gilded mirror in my bathing chamber and study the girl in the reflection.

"Perfect," Hiln says.

The other maids are silent, their eyes drawn again and again to the lace gown they helped dress me in. I don't blame them. Vasna may be poor, but her lacemakers are unparalleled. Those makers wove a masterpiece for me with threads as thin as spider silk and dyed a brilliant sapphire, the color a nod to my magic.

It's also an exact match for the jewel the king gave me.

To my surprise, Hiln didn't jerk my hair into another headache-inducing updo. Instead, she only drew enough back from my face to fasten a traditional Vasnan hairpiece of flowers and feathers over one ear. The rest she left in long, glossy waves down my back. Militant as she is, I can't help appreciating her work. My saltwater-beaten hair has never shone like it does now.

"Thank you," I say.

Hiln grunts and begins waving the girls out. I thank each of them as they leave, and when they're all gone, I return to the mirror, my thoughts quiet. Pensive.

The last time I wore this gown was at my presentation ball. It was a rushed affair, so the seamstresses stayed up all night sewing for me to have this dress. They wanted me to shine; they wanted Vasna to shine. I run my hands down the bodice, remembering with a sad smile how Selena and I brought them all tea in the wee hours of the morning, how we offered to help but were shooed away instead.

Now I wear their work here, in the dragon kingdom. I wonder if they ever thought these threads would travel so far. I certainly didn't. All my life, I thought I'd stay in Vasna.

The night my power awakened changed that. It changed everything.

I'm stirred from my thoughts by a knocking in the room beyond. My skirts softly swishing about me, I go to the bedchamber. Another knock sounds, and this time, I'm able to identify the source.

It came from the hidden door, the one between the king's chamber and mine. My quiet heart now thuds against my ribcage.

It's him.

I'm suddenly filled with a dozen different worries—Will he like my gown? My hair? Me? I don't know, but what I do know is I shouldn't be this nervous. This soon-to-be-marriage is a political one, not one of two starry-eyed lovers infatuated with another. It's better to stay levelheaded. Why do I have to keep reminding myself of that?

A third knock, this one more urgent, is loud enough to rattle the wall.

I only need to recall the last door that wasn't answered quickly enough to find myself snatching this one open.

On the other side, Rally stands with a fist raised and ready for more knocking.

"My apologies, Your Highness." He drops into a hasty bow. Behind him, Ty does the same. "We were told you were ready."

"No apology is needed," I say, equal parts relieved and disappointed not to see the king. "I am ready. Will His Majesty not be escorting me this evening?" My eyes sweep over the brothers' formal wear.

"I'm afraid not," Rally says. "He does apologize that he could not meet you here."

He offers an arm, and I summon the most gracious smile I can muster. "I'm sure it's been an eventful day for him. I would be most grateful for your escort." I take his arm, and he shuts the door behind us.

"I know I'm a poor substitute," he says, "but at least you don't have to walk with Ty."

His brother responds with yet another crude gesture from what I begin to think is an endless repository.

***

We near the banquet hall right as night is falling. The first stars are emerging, and truthfully, I'd rather run outside the city and see them than face what I'm about to walk into.

Nonsense, I tell myself as we approach the golden light within and the rising swell of voices. *You've been in front of plenty of crowds. True, none of them were as large as this is likely to be, and none of them consisted of dragons, but...*

I run out of consolations rather quickly.

"I hope you'll excuse my forwardness Your Highness," Rally says as the pair of guards blocking the entrance step aside, "but might I offer a word of advice?"

My pulse quickens as I take in the crowd within. There are *hundreds* here. Any second and they'll spot us. "Of course." Ty stands beside me, his expression sober.

"In truth, the advice is from my wife. She's also human."

I glance at him in surprise. "Then her words will be even more welcome."

"She would say that dragons and men are not so different, but when it comes to women, they're no different at all."

Ty, eyes twinkling with mischief, knocks one fist against a raised finger on the other hand.

"They're fools," Rally interprets.

I smile at the pair of them. "I would like to meet your wife."

"She would like that as well."

"Until then, please give her my thanks."

Rally inclines his head and ushers me into the room.

Like a spell, the entire hall falls utterly silent. Every eye turns our way, and I fight not to buckle under the weight of their scrutiny.

I am a princess of Vasna, I tell myself, taking strength from the gown woven by hands that love me.

I lift my chin and observe the room in a casual way, as if I see such opulence every day. Clusters of sumptuous settees are arranged in half-moon shapes near the walls, and at the center of each, a brazier table, the coals within glowing softly, warms the glistening dishes on top.

The room's middle remains clear, and servants pass to and fro with heavy-laden trays. Or they would, if they weren't also stopped and staring.

As if by a silent command, they stand aside, clearing a path to the hall's far end where, seated alone on a raised dais, the Dragon King waits.

When his eyes meet mine, I could swear my heart stops.

"He'll come for you," Rally whispers, and then he and his brother retreat into the shadows, leaving me to face the crowd alone.

No, not alone. The king stands, and as soon as he does, every head lowers. His gaze and his alone remains on me.

A fire lights in his eyes as he steps off the dais and starts toward me. This is different than the blaze I saw when he threatened Abely, and I feel the heat of it shiver through me as he stalks my way, the floor shuddering impossibly beneath his steps as his subjects wait.

I hold my skirts out at my sides and curtsy as he closes in. "Your Majesty," I say in a breathy voice.

"They didn't tell me you were wearing that."

My throat is suddenly very dry.

That was not the reaction I was hoping for.

"Is something wrong with it, Your Majesty?" I ask, peering up at him.

The fire in his eyes blazes high. Then he blinks, and the flames vanish.

"Of course not," he says.

Instead of an arm, he holds his hand out to me. I take it and try to ignore the sting of disappointment.

"Please join me," the king booms, "in welcoming Princess Serah Celandina to the Kingdom of Tirenth."

"Welcome," his court says in unison, their heads still bowed. I'm sure the greeting isn't *meant* to be unsettling.

Together, the king and I walk the length of the silent hall together. He's wearing the coat I chose for him—a long, open dress coat with silver embroidery along the lapels and edges—and I can't deny he looks handsome in it.

All right, strikingly handsome.

Well, his lack of courtesy is no excuse for my own.

"You look dashing," I whisper.

His fingers tighten on mine. "Thank you."

At his bewildered tone, I sneak a glance at him. Is he...blushing? Surely not.

"Did you polish your horns?" I ask. "They seem to be gleaming more than usual."

"I did."

He is *definitely* blushing.

My cheeks pucker in an effort not to smile. I've blushed more in the past couple of days than I have in my entire life, and to return the favor almost makes up for his reaction to my gown.

The king guides me onto the dais first and draws me down beside him. When we're both seated, the hall finally returns to life. I breathe a sigh of relief as dishes begin clattering again.

Servants descend upon us, and in seconds, a vast array of meats, breads, and dips engulf the table. At a gesture from the king, I make the first selection. Some moments pass before he speaks.

"How was your time with my sister?"

It's not the question I expected first, but I appreciate the attempt at conversation. "Wonderful. We spent a lovely afternoon together."

He speaks little after that and looks at me even less. I occupy myself for some time by surreptitiously observing those around us. In appearance, no one seems anything but human, but I notice suggestions of their other forms—hair sculpted into the shape of horns, bracelets crafted to look like scales.

Strangely, no one but servants approach. There are no greetings or introductions. In truth, I feel a bit like a possession on display.

A not-so-favored one at that.

When music begins, I realize there's to be dancing. A sweet, verdant scent fills the air as servants begin opening the arched doors looking out onto a lush garden painted silver in the moonlight. The king sighs like someone bereft of all hope.

"Will you dance with me?" he asks.

I wipe my fingers with a napkin. "Can you bear it?"

His head whips my way. "What?"

"Dancing with me." I meet his shocked gaze. "I don't mean to sound churlish. It's just that I'm not sure my company is pleasing to you this evening."

His jaw works. "You misunderstand me, Princess." Abruptly, he shoots to his feet and holds his hand out. "Please dance with me."

I consider the hand a second longer than I likely should with everyone watching. In the end, I take it, of course. What else can I do?

Besides, pathetic as it may be, I really do want to dance with him.

The room comes to a standstill once more as he leads me out onto the floor. All eyes are on us.

"Do you happen to know the evocation?" he asks.

My lips smile of their own accord. This is one area of my Tirenthian tutelage that was not neglected. "I do, Your Majesty."

The evocation is one of the dragon kingdom's oldest dances, a moderately-paced, graceful dance meant to mimic two bodies in flight. I could trace the steps in my sleep.

Yes, I could definitely do that if the king wasn't slipping his hand around my waist at this very moment, his touch sending a quiver down my side.

The orchestra strikes up the music—a single, long note held like an ascent—and then we begin to move as the melody dips and climbs.

The king's movements are flawless. Precise. He leads with confidence, guiding me in a tight circle so that others may join, and now that we've begun, they do. The hall is soon filled with whirling couples, though they continue to give us a wide berth.

"Where did you learn this dance?" the king asks. He twirls me away from him and draws me back again, my gown flaring around us. "I'll assume it wasn't from our minister."

"You aren't still angry with him?"

"I am."

Best to leave that be, then. "My dance instructor. He insisted I know traditional dances from every kingdom on the continent for my presentation ball."

The tempo picks up, and we're silent as we perform the more complex footwork of the dance's midpoint. A step forward, a step back, two to the side and a brush step back again—we whirl and embrace, every motion as fluid as if we've danced together for years. I see my own satisfaction reflected in the king's eyes.

That's probably to blame for what I say next.

"It's a shame you couldn't attend," I say, glancing up at him. "My ball, that is."

He doesn't respond, yet his gaze remains fixed on mine. The song is nearing its end, and I wonder if he's going to answer at all when he lifts the hand from my waist in signal to the orchestra. The music slows.

"Did you wear this same dress?" he asks, his hand tracing its way around my hip.

We're barely swaying, and yet I feel as if I can't breathe. "I did, Your Majesty."

"You might think it better that I didn't come then."

His lips arc into a hungry smile.

"I might have stolen you away on sight."

Before I can find my voice, he raises his hand again, and the music slows. An arm encircles me, drawing me closer.

"I thought you didn't care for it," I breathe as he intertwines his fingers with mine.

"Would you be angry if I said it wasn't really the gown I was interested in?"

A delighted laugh escapes my lips. "No, Your Majesty."

We move across the room in a gentle rhythm, the music soft and steady. I try smiling at a couple of the nearby ladies, but their eyes flit away.

"Tell me about this ball of yours," the king says. "What was it for?"

"It's Vasnan tradition to hold a ball when a woman is ready to present herself as eligible for marriage. We call them balls, but that's really due to the continent's influence. They're rather informal and held on the beach."

"All Vasnan women do this when they come of age?"

"Most of them do."

"And when is marrying age, Princess?"

"Twenty is tradition, though some girls prefer earlier."

"But not you?"

I glance off past his shoulder. "No. I waited."

"Was there someone you were waiting for?"

Do I imagine his voice darkening? I peek up at him, but his own eyes are tracking something over my head.

"No, Your Majesty. I simply didn't wish to leave home."

"It must be difficult for you then, coming here."

"I'm hopeful Tirenth will become just as dear to me, Your Majesty."

"Soren," he says.

"Pardon?"

My breath catches as his gaze falls on mine, seizing it in a decisive grip.

"Soren," he repeats. "'Your Majesty' is for others. Not for you."

I wet my lips. "I was told not to call you…"

"And I'm telling you differently."

He spins me in a slow circle before sweeping me back into his arms. "What will you miss most?"

"Miss?" I'm so flustered I can't even remember what we were talking about.

He wants me to call him by his *given name*. Even if he wasn't a dragon, a human king would hardly offer that.

"About Vasna," he says.

"Oh." This I can answer. "My little sister."

"The one who threatened me?"

I bite back a laugh. "Yes, the one who threatened you."

"After the ceremony, she's welcome to visit you any time you like."

"Thank you. I'm sure she will."

"Once your mother decides I have no intention of eating you?"

This time I can't restrain my laughter. "Yes, Your—"

He lifts a brow at me.

"Yes, Soren."

A flame sparks in his eyes, there and gone again.

The music quickens, and we glide in skipping steps around the perimeter of the dance floor. Afterward, when my cheeks are flushed and my heart is racing, I experience another wild impulse.

"Why didn't you escort me here this evening?" I blurt out.

The words are barely out of my mouth before I regret them. Have I lost my head? He only just offered me his name, and I'm chiding him?

The music has slowed again to give those dancing a chance to catch their breath, and though the king—*Soren*—hardly seems winded, he waits a long time before responding.

"I went to see the wyverns," he says.

"Oh, of course." I smile, eager to put my foolishness behind us. "Forgive me, I didn't realize—"

"I went to see the wyverns in my first form. And I was not fit to see you for some time."

His *first* form. Even as he says it, his body tenses. I lift my eyes in search of his, but his gaze has turned distant. Steely.

Does he think I fear his other self?

Perhaps I should. Perhaps it's rational to fear a dragon, but I'm struggling to find any rationality just now.

"I'm not afraid to see you as you are," I say.

His foot tangles in my gown, nearly tripping us both. He rights us, but his eyes are round and unbelieving at his clumsiness.

I believe it may be the first time in his life he's stumbled.

"I apologize, Princess."

"It's quite all right."

His silence continues through another circuit around the room. We're halfway through the next when he says, "I don't fear you seeing me as I am." He unfurls me in a long, measured rotation before drawing our bodies back together and holding us there. "I am king. I must walk the line between man and beast, and my first form is not so easily controlled."

The world falls away as he catches my chin between thumb and forefinger.

"Especially when it comes to my mate."

I catch a glimpse then of that other self. His gaze is a storm of emotion, a tempest drawing me in.

"You barely know me," I hear myself say.

The storm's call only intensifies.

The reasonable lady I'm meant to be would plant her heels and resist that draw, but if dragons are fools, I suppose I am, too.

Because I lean in.

I let him pull me near. I relish his grasp on me as desire rages in his eyes. When he bends lower, I tilt my face to him, my own eyes fluttering shut to welcome the torrent.

"Serah!"

Did someone call me?

"Serah, Serah!"

My eyes spring open, and the king's hand on me withdraws. A beaming Lady Tilanthia swings into my line of vision to clutch my arm.

"Serah, I *must* speak with you." She turns a pleading glance on her brother. "You don't mind, do you?"

It's then that I realize just how many attendees are watching us. As soon as they see I've noticed, however, they spin away.

Embarrassment may just swallow me whole.

I forget all that, though, as the king says, "You may borrow her, Tilly, as long as the lady is willing to continue our discussion afterward."

My face is aflame, but the reply thrills me to my toes.

Mumbling something incoherent, I allow Lady Tilanthia to drag me aside.

"He's here," she squeals through her fingers.

"Who?" I barely know where I am.

"Who?" she repeats in astonishment. "Lord Lyken."

Oh dear. A quick glance behind her shows me the king now engaged in conversation with several nobles. Was I what was keeping them away?

"Where is he?" I ask. Maybe she'll be satisfied with a few furtive looks at him, and I can be on my way. I'm eager to get back to the king.

Soren. I'm eager to get back to Soren.

"Just outside, in the gardens." She sinks her teeth into her lip. "Will you come with me to talk to him?"

I almost let out a groan, and I think I would if she didn't look so desperate.

"All right," I say, "but what excuse will I use?"

"Oh, thank you, Serah." She seizes me in a crushing hug. "Just tell him I told you about the mourning irises. Say you want to see them."

It's a believable enough ruse, so I let her drag me onward toward the open doors. I throw a final glance behind me.

His eyes snap to mine like he was only waiting for me to look back.

The gardens are cool, and while I'm sure they're beautiful, I drift through them without seeing a thing. Lady Tilanthia rattles off flower names and neighboring varieties with the same enthusiasm I often hear from Selena, who has a near identical fondness for insects. I nod and smile and wonder if my mouth will know what to do if the king comes for me again.

"Oh, Lord Lyken!"

Lady Tilanthia's greeting jolts me back to the present. Honestly, I have to admire her tact. She walked us straight to him in the most natural, guileless way possible. Even her greeting sounded genuine.

His back is toward us. He appeared to be in the midst of studying the foliage in front of him when we "stumbled" upon him, and while he smiles first at the sight of Lady Tilanthia, he startles at my presence.

"Your Highness." He bends in a deep bow, snapping an object in his palm closed as he does. A compact mirror, by the looks of it. His grin is sheepish when he rises. "I'm afraid you've caught me in a moment of vanity. I worried a bit of jute was caught in my teeth."

I'm in good humor, and I laugh like it. "A worry we've all shared."

I look to Lady Tilanthia, but she seems to have frozen. The poor thing, I wonder if this is her first infatuation.

Am I having my first as well?

I clear my throat. "Lady Tilanthia and I needed a bit of air, so she was showing me the gardens. She has a remarkable knowledge of flora. Might you show me the mourning irises she mentioned? That's the right type, isn't it, Lady Tilanthia?"

I give her an encouraging smile.

The girl dares one look at Lord Lyken. Her mouth even opens as if she's about to speak.

Then she bolts.

"I apologize, Lord Lyken," I say as she disappears around a bend. "I don't think she's feeling well."

"She is...very young."

He glances at me, and the easy understanding we experienced at our first meeting recurs. I sigh.

"I will try to speak with her."

Lord Lyken bows even lower. "I would be most grateful, for I would hate to lose my head on account of breaking the heart of the king's sister."

I can't help chuckling. "I'll speak with the king as well. I'm sure we can keep your head."

He straightens, his eyes dancing. "That's very generous, Your Highness. How can I thank you? Oh!" He holds out an elbow. "It's a paltry offering for one's head, but allow me to show you the mythical mourning iris. At the very least, it's ironic, given my good fortune."

"I thank you, but I really must get back to check on Lady Tilanthia."

He inclines his head. "Of course." His head lifts, and his smile falls.

Without warning, he strides toward me, raises his hand in a backhanded motion, and aims for my shoulder.

His eyes grow round as my wrist comes up to block him.

Shocked as I was, I reacted without a thought. Even now, I can't help thinking Mother would be proud.

"What are you doing?" I hiss. He's supposed to be my contact here, not a combatant.

He blinks at me. A finger of his outstretched hand curls against his thumb, and with obvious caution, he reaches around my raised wrist to flick something from my shoulder.

"Scorpion," he says.

My arm falls to my side. "Oh."

"They're common here."

"I see."

We stare at one another.

"Well," I say, "good evening, Lord Lyken."

"Good evening, Your Highness."

I turn to flee in the most dignified manner possible.

No, embarrassing as that was, I should thank him. I spin back around.

"Lord Ly—"

A sliver of light flashes behind him. At first, I think he's brought his mirror out again, that it's catching the moonlight.

That is until I see the figure on the balcony and the telltale curve of a drawn bow. As the arrow flies, all I can think is that I really am a fool.

A Note to You, Fair Reader

Thank you so much for giving my story a chance. I didn't know what would happen when I started posting a fantasy romance with a little Austen flair, but to my delight, there were actually readers out there who didn't mind my verbose ways.

If you enjoyed this first volume, I would be thrilled for you to leave a review on Amazon, Goodreads, and any other bookish sites you frequent. Serah and Soren's story will contain a total of three volumes, each with their own stunning cover by the talented Lulybot. You can preorder *Volume II* on Amazon, or read along as I write it at www.inkitt.com/jaylenefo rester/stories, where you can also sign up for exclusive goodies.

To stay updated on my stories, join my newsletter at www.substack.com/@jayleneforester. I would love to see you there!